KU-485-590

CONTRAST II

SHORT STORIES

DOROTHY PARKER

SAKI

compiled by
ROGER MANSFIELD
and
KEITH NEWSON

1966
THE QUEEN'S AWARD TO INDUSTRY 1966

PERGAMON PRESS

PERGAMON PRESS LTD.
OXFORD · LONDON · EDINBURGH
NEW YORK · TORONTO · SYDNEY

Copyright © 1969 Roger Mansfield and Keith Newson

First edition 1969

Library of Congress Catalog Card No. 68 – 26941

Printed in Great Britain by A. Wheaton & Co., Exeter

08 006433 7

Contents

Acknowledgements

ACKNOWLEDGEMENTS are due to Methuen & Co. Ltd., London, for their kind permission to include eight stories from *The Best of Dorothy Parker*.

Introduction

DOROTHY PARKER and Saki (Hector Munro) were both professional writers – journalists, reviewers, commentators – whose short stories became very well known to the general public for their humour, their readability, and their entertaining views of the societies of which the authors were a part. Of course, the worlds they lived in and wrote about were different: Saki belonged to a prosperous middle class in Edwardian England, Dorothy Parker to the cosmopolitan background of New York between the two World Wars. Their styles of writing are typical of their different backgrounds, and they have different approaches to the technique of short story writing.

But, in selecting stories for this "Contrast" volume, we became aware of much common ground between the authors. For each was a satirist, with an alert ear and a sharp tongue, ready to deflate the pompous or unmask the hypocrite. The prejudice and narrow-mindedness of many prosperous people leading all too comfortable, ordered and dull lives, are exposed as effectively in Dorothy Parker's 'Clothe the Naked' or 'Arrangement in Black and White' as in Saki's 'The Mappined Life' or 'The Lumber Room'. And these are comments on life still valid in western society today.

When Dorothy Parker died in 1967 at the age of 73, *The Times* obituary notice described her as a 'writer of disenchanted short stories, poet, scriptwriter and legendary wit' whose work 'was characterised by brilliant humour and teasing cynicism'. Some of her witticisms have passed almost into proverbs, such as the couplet:

> 'Men seldom make passes
> At girls who wear glasses'

and all her stories in this selection have this quality of 'teasing cynicism'. One shudders at the poverty of the personal relationships in 'The Waltz', 'Too Bad', 'Here We Are', 'You Were Perfectly Fine' or 'Arrangement in Black and White'. But how accurately she has represented the accents, the attitudes, of the characters here! This is what makes the stories so funny and so real. There is sentiment, too, verging perhaps on sentimentality in a story like 'Clothe the Naked'; but this only reinforces our impression of Dorothy Parker's genuine humanity. 'Horsie' veers us so gently, so subtly, from laughter to pathos: who really deserves our respect in the end – surely not the cold, shallow, wealthy couple or their pampered child?

It is in drawing characters that Dorothy Parker excels: in this selection perhaps only 'Clothe the Naked' depends for its effect upon its construction. Saki, however, represents the other kind of short story writer, who subordinates character to plot, and hopes to catch us unawares with the twist at the end. The art here, of course, is to draw a character just complex enough to surprise us without straining our credulity too far: 'Tobermory' must remain cat enough to be slaughtered by an ordinary tom; and Egbert's marriage in 'The Reticence of Lady Anne' has to be hollow enough to make it possible for him to take the corpse of his wife for the living reality. Only the lack of love and understanding in Conradin's home can make his terrible revenge on his aunt (whom Saki modelled on his own Aunt Augusta, one of the two fiercesome ladies who brought up the Munro children in North Devon) credible or acceptable, in the story of 'Sredni Vashtar'.

Hector Munro was born in 1870, and in the pre-1914 years established for himself a reputation as a cultivated conversationalist, much travelled as a newspaper correspondent, excellent company in the club or the middle-class drawing-room; but he remained a lonely and detached figure until his death in action in No-man's-land in 1916, a bachelor and a cynic, who developed in some of his later stories a new note of seriousness. 'The Philanthropist and the Happy Cat' and 'Morlvera', for instance, are deeper comments on the social scene of Edwardian England than the earlier story, 'The Mouse'. But all these stories are good entertainment in that they are prepared to turn the values of that strict society inside out for comic effect, while still in style and manners retaining the characteristic flavour of the period.

In style, Dorothy Parker and Saki are clearly contrasted. Parker's writing is obviously American, colloquial and normally direct. Saki's vocabulary and sentence structures are characteristic of his more leisurely time and his cultivated social background. Their characters, too, are typical of the authors' own environments – many of Dorothy Parker's women seem to have an aggressive self-confidence that supports the English prejudice about American ladies; and Saki's men are surprisingly like the typical English gentlemen that recur in American films. Yet they have in common an accurate ear for people's conversation, and an ability to turn a phrase to a witty conclusion: Jocantha in 'The Philanthropist and the Happy Cat' 'upset a milk-jug and swore at it daintily'; and the bride in 'Here We Are' 'had been staring raptly out of the window, drinking in the big weathered signboards that extolled the phenomena of codfish without bones and screens no rust could corrupt'.

We have put these stories together, therefore, because we believe them to be not only entertaining in their own right, but also all the richer in significance and interest for being compared and contrasted. For young readers today, neither writer presents a contemporary scene, yet we believe that the authors have in common such a genuine human interest and insight into the weaknesses of our fellow-men, that their stories remain as relevant, thought-provoking and enjoyable as when they were first written.

ROGER MANSFIELD
KEITH NEWSON

THE TRUTH

The Waltz

WHY, *thank you so much, I'd adore to.*

I don't want to dance with him. I don't want to dance with anybody. And even if I did, it wouldn't be him. He'd be well down among the last ten. I've seen the way he dances; it looks like something you do on Saint Walpurgis Night. Just think, not a quarter of an hour ago, here I was sitting, feeling so sorry for the poor girl he was dancing with. And now *I'm* going to be the poor girl. Well, well. Isn't it a small world?

And a peach of a world, too. A true little corker. Its events are so fascinatingly unpredictable, are not they? Here I was, minding my own business, not doing a stitch of harm to any living soul. And then he comes into my life, all smiles and city manners, to sue me for the favour of one memorable mazurka. Why, he scarcely knows my name, let alone what it stands for. It stands for Despair, Bewilderment, Futility, Degradation, and Premeditated Murder, but little does he wot. I don't wot his name, either; I haven't any idea what it is. Jukes, would be my guess from the look in his eyes. How do you do, Mr Jukes? And how is that dear little brother of yours, with the two heads?

Ah, now why did he have to come around me, with his low requests? Why can't he let me lead my own life? I ask so little – just to be left alone in my quiet corner of the table, to do my evening brooding over all my sorrows. And he must come, with his bows and his scrapes and his may-I-have-this-ones. And I had to go and tell him that I'd adore to dance with him. I cannot understand why I wasn't struck right down dead. Yes, and being struck dead would look like a day in the country, compared to struggling out a dance with this boy. But what could

I do? Everyone else at the table had got up to dance, except him and me. There was I, trapped. Trapped like a trap in a trap.

What can you say, when a man asks you to dance with him? I most certainly will *not* dance with you, I'll see you in hell first. Why, thank you, I'd like to awfully, but I'm having labour pains. Oh, yes, *do* let's dance together – it's so nice to meet a man who isn't a scaredy-cat about catching my beri-beri. No. There was nothing for me to do, but say I'd adore to. Well, we might as well get it over with. All right, Cannonball, let's run out on the field. You won the toss; you can lead.

Why, I think it's more of a waltz, really. Isn't it? We might just listen to the music a second. Shall we? Oh, yes, it's a waltz. Mind? Why, I'm simply thrilled. I'd love to waltz with you.

I'd love to waltz with you. I'd love to waltz with you. I'd love to have my tonsils out. I'd love to be in a midnight fire at sea. Well, it's too late now. We're getting under way. *Oh.* Oh, dear. Oh, dear, dear, dear. Oh, this is even worse than I thought it would be. I suppose that's the one dependable law of life – everything is always worse than you thought it was going to be. Oh, if I had any real grasp of what this dance would be like, I'd have held out for sitting it out. Well, it will probably amount to the same thing in the end. We'll be sitting it out on the floor in a minute, if he keeps this up.

I'm so glad I brought it to his attention that this is a waltz they're playing. Heaven knows what might have happened, if he had thought it was something fast; we'd have blown the sides right out of the building. Why does he always want to be somewhere that he isn't? Why can't we stay in one place just long enough to get acclimated? It's this constant rush, rush, rush, that's the curse of American life. That's the reason that we're all of us so – *Ow!* For God's sake, don't *kick*, you idiot; this is only second down. Oh, my shin. My poor, poor shin, that I've had ever since I was a little girl!

Oh, no, no, no. Goodness, no. It didn't hurt the least little bit.

And anyway it was my fault. Really it was. Truly. Well, you're just being sweet, to say that. It really was all my fault.

I wonder what I'd better do – kill him this instant, with my naked hands, or wait and let him drop in his traces. Maybe it's best not to make a scene. I guess I'll just lie low, and watch the pace get him. He can't keep this up indefinitely – he's only flesh and blood. Die he must, and die he shall, for what he did to me. I don't want to be of the over-sensitive type, but you can't tell me that kick was unpremeditated. Freud says there are no accidents. I've led no cloistered life, I've known dancing partners who have spoiled my slippers and torn my dress; but when it comes to kicking, I am Outraged Womanhood. When you kick me in the shin, *smile*.

Maybe he didn't do it maliciously. Maybe it's just his way of showing his high spirits. I suppose I ought to be glad that one of us is having such a good time. I suppose I ought to think myself lucky if he brings me back alive. Maybe it's captious to demand of a practically strange man that he leave your shins as he found them. After all, the poor boy's doing the best he can. Probably he grew up in the hill country, and never had no larnin'. I bet they had to throw him on his back to get shoes on him.

Yes, it's lovely, isn't it? It's simply lovely. It's the loveliest waltz. Isn't it? Oh, I think it's lovely, too.

Why, I'm getting positively drawn to the Triple Threat here. He's my hero. He has the heart of a lion, and the sinews of a buffalo. Look at him – never a thought of the consequences, never afraid of his face, hurling himself into every scrimmage, eyes shining, cheeks ablaze. And shall it be said that I hung back? No, a thousand times no. What's it to me if I have to spend the next couple of years in a plaster cast? Come on, Butch, right through them! Who wants to live for ever?

Oh. Oh, dear. Oh, he's all right, thank goodness. For a while I thought they'd have to carry him off the field. Ah, I couldn't bear to have anything happen to him. I love him. I love him better than anybody in the world. Look at the spirit he gets into a dreary, commonplace waltz; how effete the other dancers seem, beside him. He is youth and vigour and courage, he is strength and gaiety and – *Ow!* Get off my instep, you hulking peasant! What do you think I am, anyway – a gangplank? *Ow!*

No, of course it didn't hurt. Why, it didn't a bit. Honestly. And it was all my fault. You see, that little step of yours – well, it's perfectly lovely, but it's just a tiny bit tricky to follow at first. Oh, did you work it up yourself? You really did? Well, aren't you amazing! Oh, now I think I've got it. Oh, I think it's lovely. I was watching you do it when you were dancing before. It's awfully effective when you look at it.

It's awfully effective when you look at it. I bet I'm awfully effective when you look at me. My hair is hanging along my cheeks, my skirt is swaddling about me, I can feel the cold damp of my brow. I must look like something out of the 'Fall of the House of Usher'. This sort of thing takes a fearful toll of a woman my age. And he worked up his little step himself, he with his degenerate cunning. And it was just a tiny bit tricky at first, but now I think I've got it. Two stumbles, slip, and a twenty-yard dash; yes, I've got it. I've got several other things, too, including a split shin and a bitter heart. I hate this creature I'm chained to. I hated him the moment I saw his leering, bestial face. And here I've been locked in his noxious embrace for the thirty-five years this waltz has lasted. Is that orchestra never going to stop playing? Or must this obscene travesty of a dance go on until hell burns out?

Oh, they're going to play another encore. Oh, goody. Oh, that's lovely. Tired? I should say I'm not tired. I'd like to go on like this forever.

I should say I'm not tired. I'm dead, that's all I am. Dead, and in what a cause! And the music is never going to stop playing, and we're going on like this, Double-Time Charlie and I, throughout eternity. I suppose I won't care any more, after the first hundred thousand years. I suppose nothing will matter then, not heat nor pain nor broken heart nor cruel, aching weariness. Well. It can't come too soon for me.

I wonder why I didn't tell him I was tired. I wonder why I didn't suggest going back to the table. I could have said let's just listen to the music. Yes, and if he would, that would be the first bit of attention he has given it all evening. George Jean Nathan said that the lovely rhythms of the waltz should be listened to in stillness and not be accompanied by strange gyrations of the human body. I think that's what he said. I think it was George Jean Nathan. Anyhow, whatever he said and whoever he was and whatever he's doing now, he's better off than I am. That's safe. Anybody who isn't waltzing with this Mrs O'Leary's cow I've got here is having a good time.

Still if we were back at the table, I'd probably have to talk to him. Look at him – what could you say to a thing like that! Did you go to the circus this year, what's your favourite kind of ice-cream, how do you spell cat? I guess I'm as well off here. As well off as if I were in a cement mixer in full action.

I'm past all feeling now. The only way I can tell when he steps on me is that I can hear the splintering of bones. And all the events of my life are passing before my eyes. There was the time I was in a hurricane in the West Indies, there was the day I got my head cut open in the taxi smash, there was the night the drunken lady threw a bronze ash-tray at her own true love and got me instead, there was that summer that the sailboat kept capsizing. Ah, what an easy, peaceful time was mine, until I fell in with Swifty, here. I didn't know what trouble was, before I got drawn into this *danse macabre*. I think my mind is beginning to wander. It almost seems to me as if the orchestra were stopping. It couldn't be, of course; it could never, never be. And yet in my ears there is a silence like the sound of angel voices. . . .

Oh, they've stopped, the mean things. They're not going to play any more. Oh, darn. Oh, do you think they would? Do you really think so, if you gave them twenty dollars? Oh, that would be lovely. And look, do tell them to play this same thing. I'd simply adore to go on waltzing.

Tobermory

IT WAS a chill, rain-washed afternoon of a late August day, that indefinite season when partridges are still in security or cold storage, and there is nothing to hunt – unless one is bounded on the north by the Bristol Channel, in which case one may lawfully gallop after fat red stags. Lady Blemley's house-party was not bounded on the north by the Bristol Channel, hence there was a full gathering of her guests round the tea-table on this particular afternoon. And, in spite of the blankness of the season and the triteness of the occasion, there was no trace in the company of that fatigued restlessness which means a dread of the pianola and a subdued hankering for auction bridge. The undisguised open-mouthed attention of the entire party was fixed on the homely negative personality of Mr Cornelius Appin. Of all her guests, he was the one who had come to Lady Blemley with the vaguest reputation. Someone had said he was 'clever', and he had got his invitation in the moderate expectation, on the part of his hostess, that some portion at least of his cleverness would be contributed to the general entertainment. Until tea-time that day she had been unable to discover in what direction, if any, his cleverness lay. He was neither a wit nor a croquet champion, a hypnotic force nor a begetter of amateur theatricals. Neither did his exterior suggest the sort of man in whom women are willing to pardon a generous measure of mental deficiency. He had subsided into mere Mr Appin, and the Cornelius seemed a piece of transparent baptismal bluff. And now he was claiming to have launched on the world a discovery beside which the invention of gunpowder, of the printing press, and of steam locomotion were inconsiderable trifles. Science had made bewildering strides in many directions during recent decades, but this thing seemed to belong to the demain of miracle rather than to scientific achievement.

'And do you really ask us to believe,' Sir Wilfrid was saying, 'that you have discovered a means for instructing animals in the art of human speech, and that dear old Tobermory has proved your first successful pupil?'

'It is a problem at which I have worked for the last seventeen years,' said Mr Appin, 'but only during the last eight or nine months have I been rewarded with glimmerings of success. Of course I have experimented with thousands of animals, but latterly only with cats, those wonderful creatures which have assimilated themselves so marvellously with our civilization while retaining all their highly developed feral instincts. Here and there among cats one comes across an outstanding superior intellect, just as one does among the ruck of human beings, and when I made the acquaintance of Tobermory a week ago I saw at once that I was in contact with a "Beyond-cat" of extraordinary intelligence. I had gone far along the road to success in recent experiments; with Tobermory, as you call him, I have reached the goal.'

Mr Appin concluded his remarkable statement in a voice which he strove to divest of a triumphant inflection. No one said 'Rats', though Clovis's lips moved in a monosyllabic contortion which probably invoked those rodents of disbelief.

'And do you mean to say,' asked Miss Resker, after a slight pause, 'that you have taught Tobermory to say and understand easy sentences of one syllable?'

'My dear Miss Resker,' said the wonder-worker patiently, 'one teaches little children and savages and backward adults in that piecemeal fashion; when one has once solved the problem of making a beginning with an animal of highly developed intelligence one has no need for those halting methods. Tobermory can speak our language with perfect correctness.'

This time Clovis very distinctly said, 'Beyond-rats!' Sir Wilfrid was more polite, but equally sceptical.

'Hadn't we better have the cat in and judge for ourselves?' suggested Lady Blemley.

Sir Wilfrid went in search of the animal, and the company settled themselves down to the languid expectation of witnessing some more or less adroit drawing-room ventriloquism.

In a minute Sir Wilfrid was back in the room, his face white beneath its tan and his eyes dilated with excitement.

'By Gad, it's true!'

His agitation was unmistakably genuine, and his hearers started forward in a thrill of awakened interest.

Collapsing into an armchair he continued breathlessly: 'I found him dozing in the smoking-room, and called out to him to come for his tea. He blinked at me in his usual way, and I said, "Come on, Toby; don't keep us waiting"; and, by Gad! he drawled out in a most horribly natural voice that he'd come when he dashed well pleased! I nearly jumped out of my skin!'

Appin had preached to absolutely incredulous hearers; Sir Wilfrid's statement carried instant conviction. A Babel-like chorus of startled exclamation arose, amid which the scientist sat mutely enjoying the first fruit of his stupendous discovery.

In the midst of the clamour Tobermory entered the room and made his way with velvet tread and studied unconcern across to the group seated round the tea-table.

A sudden hush of awkwardness and constraint fell on the company. Somehow there seemed an element of embarrassment in addressing on equal terms a domestic cat of acknowledged dental ability.

'Will you have some milk, Tobermory?' asked Lady Blemley in a rather strained voice.

'I don't mind if I do,' was the response, couched in a tone of even indifference. A shiver of suppressed excitement went through the listeners, and Lady Blemley might be excused for pouring out the saucerful of milk rather unsteadily.

'I'm afraid I've spilt a good deal of it,' she said apologetically.

'After all, it's not my Axminster,' was Tobermory's rejoinder.

Another silence fell on the group, and then Miss Resker, in her best district-visitor manner, asked if the human language had been difficult to learn. Tobermory looked squarely at her for a moment and then fixed his gaze serenely on the middle distance. It was obvious that boring questions lay outside his scheme of life.

'What do you think of human intelligence?' asked Mavis Pellington lamely.

'Of whose intelligence in particular?' asked Tobermory coldly.

'Oh, well, mine for instance,' said Mavis with a feeble laugh.

'You put me in an embarrassing position,' said Tobermory, whose tone and attitude certainly did not suggest a shred of embarrassment. 'When your inclusion in this house-party was suggested Sir Wilfrid protested that you were the most brainless woman of his acquaintance, and that there was a wide distinction between hospitality and the care of the feeble-minded. Lady Blemley replied that your lack of brain-power was the precise quality which had earned you your invitation, as you were the only person she could think of who might be idiotic enough to buy their old car. You know, the one they call "The Envy of Sisyphus", because it goes quite nicely up-hill if you push it.'

Lady Blemley's protestations would have had greater effect if she had not casually suggested to Mavis only that morning that the car in question would be just the thing for her down at her Devonshire home.

Major Barfield plunged in heavily to effect a diversion.

'How about your carryings-on with the tortoise-shell puss up at the stables, eh?'

The moment he had said it everyone realized the blunder.

'One does not usually discuss these matters in public,' said Tobermory frigidly. 'From a slight observation of your ways since you've been in this house I should imagine you'd find it inconvenient if I were to shift the conversation on to your own little affairs.'

The panic which ensued was not confined to the Major.

'Would you like to go and see if cook has got your dinner

ready?' suggested Lady Blemley hurriedly, affecting to ignore the fact that it wanted at least two hours to Tobermory's dinner-time.

'Thanks,' said Tobermory, 'not quite so soon after my tea. I don't want to die of indigestion.'

'Cats have nine lives, you know,' said Sir Wilfrid heartily.

'Possibly,' answered Tobermory; 'but only one liver.'

'Adelaide!' said Mrs Cornett, 'do you mean to encourage that cat to go out and gossip about us in the servants' hall?'

The panic had indeed become general. A narrow ornamental balustrade ran in front of most of the bedroom windows at the Towers, and it was recalled with dismay that this had formed a favourite promenade for Tobermory at all hours, whence he could watch the pigeons – and heaven knew what else besides. If he intended to become reminiscent in his present outspoken strain the effect would be something more than disconcerting. Mrs Cornett, who spent much time at her toilet table, and whose complexion was reputed to be of a nomadic though punctual disposition, looked as ill at ease as the Major. Miss Scrawen, who wrote fiercely sensuous poetry and led a blameless life, merely displayed irritation; if you are methodical and virtuous in private you don't necessarily want everyone to know it. Bertie van Tahn, who was so depraved at seventeen that he had long ago given up trying to be any worse, turned a dull shade of gardenia white, but he did not commit the error of dashing out of the room like Odo Finsberry, a young gentleman who was understood to be reading for the Church and who was possibly disturbed at the thought of scandals he might hear concerning other people. Clovis had the presence of mind to maintain a composed exterior; privately he was calculating how long it would take to procure a box of fancy mice through the agency of the *Exchange and Mart* as a species of hush-money.

Even in a delicate situation like the present, Agnes Resker could not endure to remain too long in the background.

'Why did I ever come down here?' she asked dramatically.

Tobermory immediately accepted the opening.

'Judging by what you said to Mrs Cornett on the croquet-lawn yesterday, you were out for food. You described the Blemleys as the dullest people to stay with that you knew, but said they were clever enough to employ a first-rate cook; otherwise they'd find it difficult to get anyone to come down a second time.'

'There's not a word of truth in it! I appeal to Mrs Cornett – ' exclaimed the discomfited Agnes.

'Mrs Cornett repeated your remark afterwards to Bertie van Tahn,' continued Tobermory, 'and said, "That woman is a regular Hunger Marcher; she'd go anywhere for four square meals a day," and Bertie van Tahn said – '

At this point the chronicle mercifully ceased. Tobermory had caught a glimpse of the big yellow Tom from the Rectory working his way through the shrubbery towards the stable wing. In a flash he had vanished through the open French window.

With the disappearance of his too brilliant pupil Cornelius Appin found himself beset by a hurricane of bitter upbraiding, anxious inquiry, and frightened entreaty. The responsibility for the situation lay with him, and he must prevent matters from becoming worse. Could Tobermory impart his dangerous gift to other cats? was the first question he had to answer. It was possible, he replied, that he might have initiated his intimate friend the stable puss into his new accomplishment, but it was unlikely that his teaching could have taken a wider range as yet.

'Then,' said Mrs Cornett, 'Tobermory may be a valuable cat and a great pet; but I'm sure you'll agree, Adelaide, that both he and the stable cat must be done away with without delay.'

'You don't suppose I've enjoyed the last quarter of an hour, do you?' said Lady Blemley bitterly. 'My husband and I are very fond of Tobermory – at least, we were before this horrible accomplishment was infused into him; but now, of course, the only thing is to have him destroyed as soon as possible.'

'We can put some strychnine in the scraps he always gets at dinner-time,' said Sir Wilfrid, 'and I will go and drown the stable cat myself. The coachman will be very sore at losing his pet, but I'll say a very catching form of mange has broken out in both cats and we're afraid of it spreading to the kennels.'

'But my great discovery!' expostulated Mr Appin; 'after all my years of research and experiment – '

'You can go and experiment on the short-horns at the farm, who are under proper control,' said Mrs Cornett, 'or the elephants at the Zoological Gardens. They're said to be highly intelligent, and they have this recommendation, that they don't come creeping about our bedrooms and under chairs, and so forth.'

An archangel ecstatically proclaiming the Millennium, and then finding that it clashed unpardonably with Henley and would have to be indefinitely postponed, could hardly have felt more crestfallen than Cornelius Appin at the reception of his wonderful achievement. Public opinion, however, was against him – in fact, had the general voice been consulted on the subject it is probable that a strong minority vote would have been in favour of including him in the strychnine diet.

Defective train arrangements and a nervous desire to see matters brought to a finish prevented an immediate dispersal of the party, but dinner that evening was not a social success. Sir Wilfrid had had rather a trying time with the stable cat and subsequently with the coachman. Agnes Resker ostentatiously limited her repast to a morsel of dry toast, which she bit as though it were a personal enemy; while Mavis Pellington maintained a vindictive silence throughout the meal. Lady Blemley kept up a flow of what she hoped was conversation, but her attention was fixed on the doorway. A plateful of carefully dosed fish scraps was in readiness on the sideboard, but sweets and savoury and dessert went their way, and no Tobermory appeared either in the dining-room or kitchen.

The sepulchral dinner was cheerful compared with the subsequent vigil in the smoking-room. Eating and drinking had at least supplied a distraction and cloak to the prevailing embarrassment. Bridge was out of the question in the general tension of nerves and tempers, and after Odo Finsberry had given a lugubrious rendering of 'Mélisande in the Wood' to a frigid audience, music was tacitly avoided. At eleven the servants went to bed, announcing that the small window in the pantry had been left open as usual for Tobermory's private use. The guests read steadily through the current batch of magazines, and fell back gradually on the 'Badminton Library' and bound volumes of *Punch*. Lady Blemley made periodic visits to the pantry, returning each time with an expression of listless depression which forestalled questioning.

At two o'clock Clovis broke the dominating silence.

'He won't turn up to-night. He's probably in the local newspaper office at the present moment, dictating the first instalment of his reminiscences. Lady What's-her-name's book won't be in it. It will be the event of the day.'

Having made this contribution to the general cheerfulness, Clovis went to bed. At long intervals the various members of the house-party followed his example.

The servants taking round early tea made a uniform announcement in reply to a uniform question. Tobermory had not returned.

Breakfast was, if anything, a more unpleasant function than dinner had been, but before its conclusion the situation was relieved. Tobermory's corpse was brought in from the shrubbery, where a gardener had just discovered it. From the bites on his throat and the yellow fur which coated his claws it was evident that he had fallen in unequal combat with the big Tom from the Rectory.

By midday most of the guests had quitted the Towers, and after lunch Lady Blemley had sufficiently recovered her spirits to write an extremely nasty letter to the Rectory, about the loss of her valuable pet.

Tobermory had been Appin's one successful pupil, and he was destined to have no successor. A few weeks later an elephant in the Dresden Zoological Garden, which had shown no previous signs of irritability, broke loose and killed an Englishman who had apparently been teasing it. The victim's name was variously reported in the papers as Oppin and Eppelin, but his front name was faithfully rendered Cornelius.

'If he was trying German irregular verbs on the poor beast,' said Clovis, 'he deserved all he got.'

Mrs Packletide's Tiger

IT WAS Mrs Packletide's pleasure and intention that she should shoot a tiger. Not that the lust to kill had suddenly descended on her, or that she felt that she would leave India safer and more wholesome than she had found it, with one fraction less of wild beast per million of inhabitants. The compelling motive for her sudden deviation towards the footsteps of Nimrod was the fact that Loona Bimberton had recently been carried eleven miles in an aeroplane by an Algerian aviator, and talked of nothing else; only a personally procured tiger-skin and a heavy harvest of Press photographs could successfully counter that sort of thing. Mrs Packletide had already arranged in her mind the lunch she would give at her house in Curzon Street, ostensibly in Loona Bimberton's honour, with a tiger-skin rug occupying most of the foreground and all of the conversation. She had also already designed in her mind the tiger-claw brooch that she was going to give Loona Bimberton on her next birthday. In a world that is supposed to be chiefly swayed by hunger and by love Mrs Packletide was an exception; her movements and motives were largely governed by dislike of Loona Bimberton.

Circumstances proved propitious. Mrs Packletide had offered a thousand rupees for the opportunity of shooting a tiger without overmuch risk or exertion, and it so happened that a neighbouring village could boast of being the favoured rendezvous of an animal of respectable antecedents, which had been driven by the increasing infirmities of age to abandon game-killing and confine its appetite to the smaller domestic animals. The prospect of earning the thousand rupees had stimulated the sporting and commercial instinct of the villagers; children were posted night and day on the outskirts of the local jungle to head the tiger back in the unlikely event of his attempting to roam away to fresh hunting-grounds, and the cheaper kinds of goats were left about with elaborate carelessness to keep him satisfied with his present quarters. The one great anxiety was lest he should die of old age before the date appointed for the memsahib's shoot. Mothers carrying their babies home through the jungle after the day's work in the fields hushed their singing lest they might curtail the restful sleep of the venerable herd-robber.

The great night duly arrived, moonlit and cloudless. A platform had been constructed in a comfortable and conveniently placed tree, and thereon crouched Mrs Packletide and her paid companion, Miss Mebbin. A goat, gifted with a particularly persistent bleat, such as even a partially deaf tiger might be reasonably expected to hear on a still night, was tethered at the correct distance. With an accurately sighted rifle and a thumb-nail pack of patience cards the sportswoman awaited the coming of the quarry.

'I suppose we are in some danger?' said Miss Mebbin.

She was not actually nervous about the wild beast, but she had a morbid dread of performing an atom more service than she had been paid for.

'Nonsense,' said Mrs Packletide; 'it's a very old tiger. It couldn't spring up here even if it wanted to.'

'If it's an old tiger I think you ought to get it cheaper. A thousand rupees is a lot of money.'

Louisa Mebbin adopted a protective elder-sister attitude towards money in general, irrespective of nationality or denomination. Her energetic intervention had saved many a rouble from dissipating itself in tips in some Moscow hotel, and francs and centimes clung to her instinctively under circumstances which would have driven them headlong from less sympathetic hands. Her speculations as to the market depreciation of tiger remnants were cut short by the appearance on the scene of the animal itself. As soon as it caught sight of the tethered goat it lay flat on the earth, seemingly less from a desire to take advantage of all available cover than for the purpose of snatching a short rest before commencing the grand attack.

'I believe it's ill,' said Louisa Mebbin, loudly in Hindustani, for the benefit of the village headman, who was in ambush in a neighbouring tree.

'Hush!' said Mrs Packletide, and at that moment the tiger commenced ambling towards his victim.

'Now, now!' urged Miss Mebbin with some excitement; 'if he doesn't touch the goat we needn't pay for it.' (The bait was an extra.)

The rifle flashed out with a loud report, and the great tawny beast sprang to one side and then rolled over in the stillness of death. In a moment a crowd of excited natives had swarmed on to the scene, and their shouting speedily carried the glad news to the village, where a thumping of tomtoms took up the chorus of triumph. And their triumph and rejoicing found a ready echo in the heart of Mrs Packletide; already that luncheon-party in Curzon Street seemed immeasurably nearer.

It was Louisa Mebbin who drew attention to the fact that the goat was in death-throes from a mortal bullet-wound, while no trace of the rifle's deadly work could be found on the tiger. Evidently the wrong animal had been hit, and the beast of prey had succumbed to heart-failure, caused by the sudden report of the rifle, accelerated by senile decay. Mrs Packletide was pardonably annoyed at the discovery; but, at any rate, she was the possessor of a dead tiger, and the villagers, anxious for their thousand rupees, gladly connived at the fiction that she had shot the beast. And Miss Mebbin was a paid companion. Therefore did Mrs Packletide face the cameras with a light heart, and her pictured fame reached from the pages of the *Texas Weekly Snapshot* to the illustrated Monday Supplement of the *Novoe Vremya*. As for Loona Bimberton, she refused to look at an illustrated paper for weeks, and her letter of thanks for the gift of a tiger-claw brooch was a model of repressed emotion. The luncheon-party she declined; there are limits beyond which repressed emotions become dangerous.

From Curzon Street the tiger-skin rug travelled down to the Manor House, and was duly inspected and admired by the county, and it seemed a fitting and appropriate thing when Mrs Packletide went to the County Costume Ball in the character of Diana. She refused to fall in, however, with Clovis's tempting suggestion of a primeval dance party, at which everyone should wear the skins of beasts they had recently slain. 'I should be in rather a Baby Bunting condition,' confessed Clovis, 'with a miserable rabbit-skin or two to wrap up in, but then,' he added with a rather malicious glance at Diana's proportions, 'my figure is quite as good as that Russian dancing boy's.'

'How amused everyone would be if they knew what really happened,' said Louisa Mebbin a few days after the ball.

'What do you mean?' asked Mrs Packletide quickly.

'How you shot the goat and frightened the tiger to death,' said Miss Mebbin, with her disagreeably pleasant laugh.

'No one would believe it,' said Mrs Packletide, her face changing colour as rapidly as though it were going through a book of patterns before post-time.

'Loona Bimberton would,' said Miss Mebbin. Mrs Packletide's face settled on an unbecoming shade of greenish white.

'You surely wouldn't give me away?' she asked.

'I've seen a week-end cottage near Dorking that I should rather like to buy,' said Miss Mebbin with seeming irrelevance. 'Six hundred and eighty, freehold. Quite a bargain, only I don't happen to have the money.'

* * *

Louisa Mebbin's pretty week-end cottage, christened by her 'Les Fauves', and gay in summer-time with its garden borders of tiger-lilies, is the wonder and admiration of her friends.

'It is a marvel how Louisa manages to do it,' is the general verdict.

Mrs Packletide indulges in no more big-game shooting.

'The incidental expenses are so heavy,' she confides to inquiring friends.

PATHETIC PEOPLE

Horsie

WHEN young Mrs Gerald Cruger came home from the hospital, Miss Wilmarth came along with her and the baby. Miss Wilmarth was an admirable trained nurse, sure and calm and tireless, with a real taste for the arranging of flowers in bowls and vases. She had never known a patient to receive so many flowers, or such uncommon ones; yellow violets and strange lilies and little white orchids poised like a bevy of delicate moths along green branches. Care and thought must have been put into their selection that they, like all the other fragile and costly things she kept about her, should be so right for young Mrs Cruger. No one who knew her could have caught up the telephone and lightly bidden the florist to deliver to her one of his five-dollar assortments of tulips, stock, and daffodils. Camilla Cruger was no complement to garden blooms.

Sometimes, when Miss Wilmarth opened the shiny boxes and carefully grouped the cards, there would come a curious expression upon her face. Playing over shorter features, it might almost have been one of wistfulness. Upon Miss Wilmarth, it served to perfect the strange resemblance that she bore through her years; her face was truly complete with that look of friendly melancholy peculiar to the gentle horse. It was not, of course, Miss Wilmarth's fault that she looked like a horse. Indeed, there was nowhere to attach any blame. But the resemblance remained.

She was tall, pronounced of bone, and erect of carriage; it was somehow impossible to speculate upon her appearance undressed. Her long face was innocent, indeed ignorant, of cosmetics, and its colour stayed steady. Confusion, heat, or haste caused her neck to flush crimson. Her mild hair was pinned with loops of nicked black wire into a narrow knot, practical to support her little high cap, like a charlotte russe from a bake-shop. She had big, trustworthy hands, scrubbed and dry, with nails cut short and so deeply cleaned with some small sharp instrument that the ends stood away from the spatulate finger-tips. Gerald Cruger, who nightly sat opposite her at his own dinner table, tried not to see her hands. It irritated him to be reminded by their sight that they must feel like straw matting and smell of white soap. For him, women who were not softly lovely were simply not women.

He tried, too, so far as it was possible to his beautiful manners, to keep his eyes from her face. Not that it was unpleasant – a kind face, certainly. But, as he told Camilla, once he looked he stayed fascinated, awaiting the toss and the whinny.

'I love horses, myself,' he said to Camilla, who lay all white and languid on her apricot satin chaise-longue. 'I'm a fool for a horse. Ah, what a noble animal, darling! All I say is, nobody has any business to go around looking like a horse and behaving as if it were all right. You don't catch horses going around looking like people, do you?'

He did not dislike Miss Wilmarth; he only resented her. He had no bad wish in the world for her, but he waited with longing the day she would leave. She was so skilled and rhythmic in her work that she disrupted the household but little. Nevertheless, her presence was an onus. There was that thing of dining with her every evening. It was a chore for him, certainly, and one that did not ease with repetition, but there was no choice. Everyone had always heard of trained nurses' bristling insistence that they be not treated as servants; Miss Wilmarth could not be asked to dine with the maids. He would not have dinner out; be away from *Camilla*? It was too much to expect the maids to institute a second dinner service or to carry trays, other than Camilla's, up and down the stairs. There were only three servants and they had work enough.

'Those children,' Camilla's mother was wont to say, chuckling. 'Those two kids. The independence of them! Struggling along on cheese and kisses. Why, they hardly let me pay for the trained nurse. And it was all we could do, last Christmas, to make Camilla take the Packard and the chauffeur.'

So Gerald dined each night with Miss Wilmarth. The small dread of his hour with her struck suddenly at him in the afternoon. He would forget it for stretches of minutes, only to be smitten sharper as the time drew near. On his way home from his office, he found grim entertainment in rehearsing his table talk, and plotting desperate innovations to it.

Cruger's Compulsory Conversations: Lesson I, a Dinner with a Miss Wilmarth, a Trained Nurse. Good evening, Miss Wilmarth. Well! And how were the patients all day? That's good, that's fine. Well! The baby gained two ounces, did she? That's fine. Yes, that's right, she will be before we know it. That's right. Well! Mrs Cruger seems to be getting stronger every day, doesn't she? That's good, that's fine. That's right, up and about before we know it. Yes, she certainly will. Well! Any visitors today? That's good. Didn't stay too long, did they? That's fine. Well! No, no, no, Miss Wilmarth – *you* go ahead. I wasn't going to say anything at all, really. No, really. Well! Well! I see where they found those two aviators after all. Yes, they certainly do run risks. That's right. Yes. Well! I see where they've been having a regular old-fashioned blizzard out West. Yes, we certainly have had a mild winter. That's right. Well! I see where they held up that jeweller's shop right in broad daylight on Fifth Avenue. Yes, I certainly don't know what we're coming to. That's right. Well! I see the cat. Do you see the cat? The cat is on the mat. It certainly is. Well! Pardon me, Miss Wilmarth, but must you look so much like a horse? Do you like to look like a horse, Miss Wilmarth? That's good, Miss Wilmarth, that's fine. You certainly do, Miss Wilmarth. That's right. Well! Will you for God's sake finish your oats, Miss Wilmarth, and let me get out of this?

Every evening he reached the dining-room before Miss Wilmarth and stared gloomily at silver and candle-flame until she was upon him. No sound of footfall heralded her coming, for her ample canvas oxfords were soled with rubber; there would be a protest of parquet, a trembling of ornaments, a creak, a rustle, and the authoritative smell of stiff linen; and there she would be, set for her ritual of evening cheer.

'Well, Mary,' she would cry to the waitress, 'you know what they say – better late than never!'

But no smile would mellow Mary's lips, no light her eyes. Mary, in converse with the cook, habitually referred to Miss Wilmarth as 'that one'. She wished no truck with Miss Wilmarth or any of the others of her guild; always in and out of a person's pantry.

Once or twice Gerald saw a strange expression upon Miss Wilmarth's face as she witnessed the failure of her adage with the maid. He could not quite classify it. Though he did not know, it was the look she sometimes had when she opened the shiny white boxes and lifted the exquisite, scentless blossoms that were sent to Camilla. Anyway, whatever it was, it increased her equine resemblance to such a point that he thought of proffering her an apple.

But she always had her big smile turned towards him when she sat down. Then she would look at the thick watch strapped to her wrist and give a little squeal that brought the edges of his teeth together.

'Mercy!' she would say. 'My good mercy! Why, I had no more idea it was so late. Well, you mustn't blame me, Mr Cruger. Don't you scold *me*. You'll just have to blame that daughter of yours. She's the one that keeps us all busy.'

'She certainly is,' he would say. 'That's right.'

He would think, and with small pleasure, of the infant Diane, pink and undistinguished and angry, among the ruffles and *choux* of her bassinet. It was her doing that Camilla had stayed so long away from him in the odorous limbo of the hospital, her doing that Camilla lay all day upon her apricot satin chaise-longue. 'We must take our time,' the doctor said, 'just ta-a-ake our ti-yem.' Yes; well, that would all be because of young Diane. It was because of her, indeed, that night upon night he must face Miss Wilmarth and comb up conversation. All right, young Diane, there you are and nothing to do about it. But you'll be an only child, young woman, that's what you'll be.

Always Miss Wilmarth followed her opening pleasantry about the baby with a companion piece. Gerald had come to know it so well he could have said it in duet with her.

'You wait,' she would say. 'Just you wait. You're the one that's going to be kept busy when the beaux start coming around. You'll see. That young lady's going to be a heart-breaker if ever I saw one.'

'I guess that's right,' Gerald would say, and he would essay a small laugh and fail at it. It made him uncomfortable, somehow embarrassed him to hear Miss Wilmarth banter of swains and conquest. It was unseemly, as rouge would have been unseemly on her long mouth and perfume on her flat bosom.

He would hurry her over to her own ground. 'Well!' he would say. 'Well! And how were the patients all day?'

But that, even with the baby's weight and the list of the day's visitors, seldom lasted past the soup.

'Doesn't that woman ever go out?' he asked Camilla. 'Doesn't our Horsie ever rate a night off?'

'Where would she want to go?' Camilla said. Her low, lazy words had always the trick of seeming a little weary of their subject.

'Well,' Gerald said, 'she might take herself a moonlight canter around the park.'

'Oh, she doubtless gets a thrill out of dining with you,' Camilla said. 'You're a man, they tell me, and she can't have seen many. Poor old horse. She's not a bad soul.'

'Yes,' he said. 'And what a round of pleasure it is, having dinner every night with Not a Bad Soul.'

'What makes you think,' Camilla said, 'that I am caught up in any whirl of gaiety, lying here?'

'Oh, darling,' he said. 'Oh, my poor darling. I didn't mean it, honestly I didn't. Oh, *Lord,* I didn't mean it. How could I complain, after all you've been through, and I haven't done a thing? Please, sweet, please. Ah, Camilla, say you know I didn't mean it.'

'After all,' Camilla said, 'you just have her at dinner. I have her around all day.'

'Sweetheart, please,' he said. 'Oh, poor angel.'

He dropped to his knees by the chaise-longue and crushed her limp, fragrant hand against his mouth. Then he remembered about being very, very gentle. He ran little apologetic kisses up and down her fingers and murmured of gardenias and lilies and thus exhausted his knowledge of white flowers.

Her visitors said that Camilla looked lovelier than ever, but they were mistaken. She was only as lovely as she had always been. They spoke in hushed voices of the new look in her eyes since her motherhood; but it was the same far brightness that had always lain there. They said how white she was and how lifted above other people; they forgot that she had always been pale as moonlight and had always worn a delicate disdain, as light as the lace that covered her breast. Her doctor cautioned tenderly against hurry, besought her to take recovery slowly – Camilla, who had never done anything quickly in her life. Her friends gathered, adoring, about the apricot satin chaise-longue where Camilla lay and moved her hands as if they hung heavy from her wrists; they had been wont before to gather and adore at the white satin sofa in the drawing-room where Camilla reclined, her hands like heavy lilies in a languid breeze. Every night, when Gerald crossed the threshold of her fragrant room, his heart leaped and his words caught in his throat; but those things had always befallen him at the sight of her. Motherhood had not brought perfection to Camilla's loveliness. She had had that before.

Gerald came home early enough, each evening, to have a while with her before dinner. He made his cocktails in her room, and watched her as she slowly drank one. Miss Wilmarth was in and out, touching flowers, patting pillows. Sometimes she brought

Diane in on display, and those would be minutes of real discomfort for Gerald. He could not bear to watch her with the baby in her arms, so acute was his vicarious embarrassment at her behaviour. She would bring her long head down close to Diane's tiny, stern face and toss it back again high on her rangy neck, all the while that strange words, in a strange high voice, came from her.

'Well, her wuzza booful dirl. Ess, her wuzza. Her wuzza, wuzza, wuzza. Ess, her *wuzz*.' She would bring the baby over to him. 'See, Daddy. Isn't us a gate, bid dirl? Isn't us booful? Say "nigh-nigh", Daddy. Us doe teepy-bye, now. Say "nigh-nigh".'

Oh, God.

Then she would bring the baby to Camilla. 'Say "nigh-nigh",' she would cry. ' "Nigh-nigh", Mummy.'

'If that brat ever calls you "Mummy",' he told Camilla once, fiercely, 'I'll turn her out in the snow.'

Camilla would look at the baby, amusement in her slow glance. 'Good night, useless,' she would say. She would hold out a finger, for Diane's pink hand to curl around. And Gerald's heart would quicken, and his eyes sting and shine.

Once he tore his gaze from Camilla to look at Miss Wilmarth, surprised by the sudden cessation of her falsetto. She was no longer lowering her head and tossing it back. She was standing quite still, looking at him over the baby; she looked away quickly, but not before he had seen that curious expression on her face again. It puzzled him, made him vaguely uneasy. That night, she made no further exhortations to Diane's parents to utter the phrase 'nigh-nigh'. In silence she carried the baby out of the room and back to the nursery.

One evening, Gerald brought two men home with him; lean, easily dressed young men, good at golf and squash rackets, his companions through his college and in his clubs. They had cocktails in Camilla's room, grouped about the chaise-longue. Miss Wilmarth, standing in the nursery adjoining, testing the temperature of the baby's milk against her wrist, could hear them all talking lightly and swiftly, tossing their sentences into the air to hang there unfinished. Now and again she could distinguish Camilla's lazy voice; the others stopped immediately when she spoke, and when she was done there were long peals of laughter. Miss Wilmarth pictured her lying there, in golden chiffon and deep lace, her light figure turned always a little away from those about her, so that she must move her head and speak her slow words over her shoulder to them. The trained nurse's face was astoundingly equine as she looked at the wall that separated them.

They stayed in Camilla's room a long time, and there was always more laughter. The door from the nursery into the hall was open, and presently she heard the door of Camilla's room being opened, too. She had been able to hear only voices before, but now she could distinguish Gerald's words as he called back from the threshold; they had no meaning to her.

'Only wait, fellers,' he said. 'Wait till you see Seabiscuit.'

He came to the nursery door. He held a cocktail shaker in one hand and a filled glass in the other.

'Oh, Miss Wilmarth,' he said. 'Oh, good evening, Miss Wilmarth. Why, I didn't know this door was open – I mean, I hope we haven't been disturbing you.'

'Oh, not the least little bit,' she said. 'Goodness.'

'Well,' he said. 'I – we were wondering if you wouldn't have a little cocktail. Won't you please?' He held out the glass to her.

'Mercy,' she said, taking it. 'Why, thank you ever so much. Thank you, Mr Cruger.'

'And, oh, Miss Wilmarth,' he said, 'would you tell Mary there'll be two more to dinner? And ask her not to have it before half an hour or so, will you? Would you mind?'

'Not the least little bit,' she said. 'Of course I will.'

'Thank you,' he said. 'Well! Thank you, Miss Wilmarth. Well! See you at dinner.'

'Thank *you*,' she said. 'I'm the one that ought to thank *you*. For the lovely little cockytail.'

'Oh,' he said, and failed at an easy laugh. He went back into Camilla's room and closed the door behind him.

Miss Wilmarth set her cocktail upon a table, and went down to inform Mary of the impending guests. She felt light and quick, and she told Mary gaily, awaiting a flash of gaiety in response. But Mary received the news impassively, made a grunt but no words, and slammed out through the swinging doors into the kitchen. Miss Wilmarth stood looking after her. Somehow servants never seemed to – She should have become used to it.

Even though the dinner hour was delayed, Miss Wilmarth was a little late. The three young men were standing in the dining-room, talking all at once and laughing all together. They stopped their noise when Miss Wilmarth entered, and Gerald moved forward to perform introductions. He looked at her, and then looked away. Prickling embarrassment tormented him. He introduced the young men, with his eyes away from her.

Miss Wilmarth had dressed for dinner. She had discarded her linen uniform and put on a frock of dark blue taffeta, cut down to a point at the neck and given sleeves that left bare the angles of her elbows. Small, stiff ruffles occurred about the hips, and the skirt was short for its year. It revealed that Miss Wilmarth had clothed her ankles in roughened grey silk and her feet in black, casket-shaped slippers, upon which little bows quivered as if in lonely terror at the expanse before them. She had been busied with her hair; it was crimped and loosened, and ends that had escaped the tongs were already sliding from their pins. All the length of her nose and chin was heavily powdered; not with a perfumed dust, tinted to praise her skin, but with coarse, bright white talcum.

Gerald presented his guests; Miss Wilmarth, Mr Minot; Miss Wilmarth, Mr Forster. One of the young men, it turned out, was Freddy, and one, Tommy. Miss Wilmarth said she was pleased to meet each of them. Each of them asked her how she did.

She sat down at the candle-lit table with the three beautiful young men. Her usual evening vivacity was gone from her. In silence she unfolded her napkin and took up her soup spoon. Her neck glowed crimson, and her face, even with its powder, looked more than ever as if it should have been resting over the top rail of a paddock fence.

'Well!' Gerald said.

'Well!' Mr Minot said.

'Getting much warmer out, isn't it?' Mr Forster said. 'Notice it?'

'It is, at that,' Gerald said. 'Well. We're about due for warm weather.'

'Yes, we ought to expect it now,' Mr Minot said. 'Any day now.'

'Oh, it'll be here,' Mr Forster said. 'It'll come.'

'I love spring,' said Miss Wilmarth. 'I just love it.'

Gerald looked deep into his soup plate. The two young men looked at her.

'Darn good time of year,' Mr Minot said. 'Certainly is.'

'And how it is!' Mr Forster said.

They ate their soup.

There was champagne all through dinner. Miss Wilmarth watched Mary fill her glass, none too full. The wine looked gay and pretty. She looked about the table before she took her first sip. She remembered Camilla's voice and the men's laughter.

'Well,' she cried. 'Here's a health, everybody!'

The guests looked at her. Gerald reached for his glass and gazed at it as intently as if he beheld a champagne goblet for the first time. They all murmured and drank.

'Well!' Mr Minot said. 'Your patients seem to be getting along pretty well, Miss Witmark. Don't they?'

'I should say they do,' she said. 'And they're pretty nice patients, too. Aren't they, Mr Cruger?'

'They certainly are,' Gerald said. 'That's right.'

'They certainly are,' Mr Minot said. 'That's what they are. Well. You must meet all sorts of people in your work, I suppose. Must be pretty interesting.'

'Oh, sometimes it is,' Miss Wilmarth said. 'It depends on the people.' Her words fell from her lips clear and separate, sterile as if each had been freshly swabbed with boracic acid solution. In her ears rang Camilla's light, insolent drawl.

'That's right,' Mr Forster said. 'Everything depends on the people, doesn't it? Always does, wherever you go. No matter what you do. Still, it must be wonderfully interesting work. Wonderfully.'

'Wonderful the way this country's come right up in medicine,' Mr Minot said. 'They tell me we have the greatest doctors in the world, right here. As good as any in Europe. Or Harley Street.'

'I see,' Gerald said, 'where they think they've found a new cure for spinal meningitis.'

'*Have* they really?' Mr Minot said.

'Yes, I saw that, too,' Mr Forster said. 'Wonderful thing. Wonderfully interesting.'

'Oh, say, Gerald,' Mr Minot said, and he went from there into an account, hole by hole, of his most recent performance at golf. Gerald and Mr Forster listened and questioned him.

The three young men left the topic of golf and came back to it again, and left it and came back. In the intervals, they related to Miss Wilmarth various brief items that had caught their eyes in the newspapers. Miss Wilmarth answered in exclamations, and turned her big smile readily to each of them. There was no laughter during dinner.

It was a short meal, as courses went. After it, Miss Wilmarth bade the guests good night and received their bows and their '*Good* night, Miss Witmark.' She said she was awfully glad to have met them. They murmured.

'Well, good night, then, Mr Cruger,' she said. 'See you tomorrow!'

'Good night, Miss Wilmarth,' Gerald said.

The three young men went and sat with Camilla. Miss Wilmarth could hear their voices and their laughter as she hung up her dark blue taffeta dress.

Miss Wilmarth stayed with the Crugers for five weeks. Camilla was pronounced well – so well that she could have dined downstairs on the last few nights of Miss Wilmarth's stay, had she been able to support the fardel of dinner at the table with the trained nurse.

'I really couldn't dine opposite that face,' she told Gerald. 'You go amuse Horsie at dinner, stupid. You must be good at it, by now.'

'All right, I will, darling,' he said. 'But God keep me, when she asks for another lump of sugar, from holding it out to her on my palm.'

'Only two more nights,' Camilla said, 'and then Thursday Nana'll be here, and she'll be gone forever.'

' "Forever", sweet, is my favourite word in the language,' Gerald said.

Nana was the round and competent Scottish woman who had nursed Camilla through her childhood and was scheduled to engineer the unknowing Diane through hers. She was a comfortable woman, easy to have in the house; a servant, and knew it.

Only two more nights. Gerald went down to dinner whistling a good old tune.

'The old grey mare, she ain't what she used to be,
Ain't what she used to be, ain't what she used to be –'

The final dinners with Miss Wilmarth were like all the others. He arrived first, and stared at the candles until she came.

'Well, Mary,' she cried on her entrance, 'you know what they say – better late than never.'

Mary, to the last, remained unamused.

Gerald was elated all the day of Miss Wilmarth's departure. He had a holiday feeling, a last-day-of-school jubilation with none of its faint regret. He left his office early, stopped at a florist's shop, and went home to Camilla.

Nana was installed in the nursery, but Miss Wilmarth had not yet left. She was in Camilla's room, and he saw her for the second time out of uniform. She wore a long brown coat and a brown rubbed velvet hat of no definite shape. Obviously, she was in the middle of the embarrassments of farewell. The melancholy of her face made it so like a horse's that the hat above it was preposterous.

'Why, there's Mr Cruger!' she cried.

'Oh, good evening, Miss Wilmarth,' he said. 'Well! Ah, hello, darling. How are you, sweet? Like these?'

He laid a florist's box in Camilla's lap. In it were strange little yellow roses, with stems and leaves and tiny, soft thorns all of blood red. Miss Wilmarth gave a little squeal at the sight of them.

'Oh, the darlings!' she cried. 'Oh, the boo-fuls!'

'And these are for you, Miss Wilmarth,' he said. He made himself face her and hold out to her a square, smaller box.

'Why, Mr Cruger,' she said. 'For me, really? Why, really, Mr Cruger.'

She opened the box and found four gardenias, with green foil and pale green ribbon holding them together.

'Oh, now, really, Mr Cruger,' she said. 'Why, I never in all my life – Oh, now, you shouldn't have done it. Really, you shouldn't. My good mercy! Well, I never saw anything so lovely in all my life. Did you, Mrs Cruger? They're *lovely*. Well, I just don't know how to *begin* to thank you. Why, I just – well, I just adore them.'

Gerald made sounds designed to convey the intelligence that he was glad she liked them, that it was nothing, that she was welcome. Her squeaks of thanks made red rise back of his ears.

'They're nice ones,' Camilla said. 'Put them on, Miss Wilmarth. And these are awfully cunning, Jerry. Sometimes you have your points.'

'Oh, I didn't think I'd *wear* them,' Miss Wilmarth said. 'I thought I'd just take them in the box like this, so they'd keep better. And it's such a nice box – I'd like to have it. I – I'd like to keep it."

She looked down at the flowers. Gerald was in sudden horror

that she might bring her head down close to them and toss it back high, crying 'wuzza, wuzza, wuzza,' at them the while.

'Honestly,' she said, 'I just can't take my eyes *off* them.'

'The woman is mad,' Camilla said. 'It's the effect of living with us, I suppose. I hope we haven't ruined you for life, Miss Wilmarth.'

'Why, Mrs Cruger,' Miss Wilmarth cried. 'Now, really! I was just telling Mrs Cruger, Mr Cruger, that I've never been on a pleasanter case. I've just had the time of my life, all the time I was here. I don't know when I – honestly, I can't stop looking at my posies, they're so lovely. Well, I just can't thank you for all you've done.'

'Well, we ought to thank you, Miss Wilmarth,' Gerald said. 'We certainly ought.'

'I really hate to say "good-bye",' Miss Wilmarth said. 'I just hate it.'

'Oh, don't say it,' Camilla said. 'I never dream of saying it. And remember, you must come in and see the baby, any time you can.'

'Yes, you certainly must,' Gerald said. 'That's right.'

'Oh, I will,' Miss Wilmarth said. 'Mercy, I just don't dare go take another look at her, or I wouldn't be able to leave, ever. Well, what am I thinking of! Why, the car's been waiting all this time. Mrs Cruger simply insists on sending me home in the car, Mr Cruger. Isn't she terrible?'

'Why, not at all,' he said. 'Why, of course.'

'Well, it's only five blocks down and over to Lexington,' she said, 'or I really couldn't think of troubling you.'

'Why, not at all,' Gerald said. 'Well! Is that where you live, Miss Wilmarth?'

She lived in some place of her own sometimes? She wasn't always disarranging somebody else's household?

'Yes,' Miss Wilmarth said. 'I have Mother there.'

Oh. Now Gerald had never thought of her having a mother. Then there must have been a father, too, some time. And Miss

Wilmarth existed because two people once had loved and known. It was not a thought to dwell upon.

'My aunt's with us, too,' Miss Wilmarth said. 'It makes it nice for Mother – you see, Mother doesn't get around very well any more. It's a little bit crowded for the three of us – I sleep on the davenport when I'm home, between cases. But it's so nice for Mother, having my aunt there.'

Even in her leisure, then, Miss Wilmarth was a disruption and a crowd. Never dwelling in a room that had been planned only for her occupancy; no bed, no corner of her own; dressing before other people's mirrors, touching other people's silver, never looking out one window that was hers. Well, doubtless she had known nothing else for so long that she did not mind or even ponder.

'Oh, yes,' Gerald said. 'Yes, it certainly must be fine for your mother. Well! Well! May I close your bags for you, Miss Wilmarth?'

'Oh, that's all done,' she said. 'The suitcase is downstairs. I'll just go get my hat-box. Well, good-bye, then, Mrs Cruger, and take care of yourself. And thank you a thousand times.'

'Good luck, Miss Wilmarth,' Camilla said. 'Come and see the baby.'

Miss Wilmarth looked at Camilla and at Gerald standing beside her, touching one long white hand. She left the room to fetch her hat-box.

'I'll take it down for you, Miss Wilmarth,' Gerald called after her.

He bent and kissed Camilla gently, very, very gently.

'Well, it's nearly over, darling,' he said. 'Sometimes I am practically convinced that there is a God.'

'It was darn decent of you to bring her gardenias,' Camilla said. 'What made you think of it?'

'I was so crazed at the idea that she was really going,' he said, 'that I must have lost my head. No one was more surprised than I, buying gardenias for Horsie. Thank the Lord she didn't put them on. I couldn't have stood that sight.'

'She's not really at her best in her street clothes,' Camilla said. 'She seems to lack a certain *chic.*' She stretched her arms slowly above her head and let them sink slowly back. 'That was a fascinating glimpse of her home life she gave us. Great fun.'

'Oh, I don't suppose she minds,' he said. 'I'll go down now and back her into the car, and that'll finish it.'

He bent again over Camilla.

'Oh, you look so lovely, sweet,' he said. 'So *lovely.*'

Miss Wilmarth was coming down the hall, when Gerald left the room, managing a pasteboard hat-box, the florist's box, and a big leather purse that had known service. He took the boxes from her, against her protests, and followed her down the stairs and out to the motor at the curb. The chauffeur stood at the open door. Gerald was glad of that presence.

'Well, good luck, Miss Wilmarth,' he said. 'And thank you so much.'

'Thank *you,* Mr Cruger,' she said. 'I – I can't tell you how I've enjoyed it all the time I was here. I never had a pleasanter – And the flowers, and everything. I just don't know what to say. I'm the one that ought to thank *you.*'

She held out her hand, in a brown cotton glove. Anyway, worn cotton was easier to the touch than dry, corded flesh. It was the last moment of her. He scarcely minded looking at the long face on the red, red neck.

'Well!' he said. 'Well! Got everything? Well, good luck, again, Miss Wilmarth, and don't forget us.'

'Oh, I won't,' she said. 'I – oh, I won't do that.'

She turned from him and got quickly into the car, to sit upright against the pale grey cushions. The chauffeur placed her hat-box at her feet and the florist's box on the seat beside her, closed the door smartly, and returned to his wheel. Gerald waved cheerily as the car slid away. Miss Wilmarth did not wave to him.

When she looked back, through the little rear window, he had already disappeared in the house. He must have run across the sidewalk – run, to get back to the fragrant room and the little yellow roses and Camilla. Their little pink baby would lie sleeping in its bed. They would be alone together; they would dine alone together by candlelight; they would be alone together in the night. Every morning and every evening Gerald would drop to his knees beside her to kiss her perfumed hand and call her sweet. Always she would be perfect, in scented chiffon and deep lace. There would be lean, easy young men, to listen to her drawl and give her their laughter. Every day there would be shiny white boxes for her, filled with curious blooms. It was perhaps fortunate that no one looked in the limousine. A beholder must have been startled to learn that a human face could look as much like that of a weary mare as did Miss Wilmarth's.

Presently the car swerved, in a turn of the traffic. The florist's box slipped against Miss Wilmarth's knee. She looked down at it. Then she took it on her lap, raised the lid a little and peeped at the waxy white bouquet. It would have been all fair then for a chance spectator; Miss Wilmarth's strange resemblance was not apparent, as she looked at her flowers. They were her flowers. A man had given them to her. She had been given flowers. They might not fade maybe for days. And she could keep the box.

The Sheep

THE enemy had declared 'no trumps'. Rupert played out his ace and king of clubs and cleared the adversary of that suit; then the Sheep, whom the Fates had inflicted on him for a partner, took the third round with the queen of clubs, and, having no other club to lead back, opened another suit. The enemy won the remainder of the tricks – and the rubber.

'I had four more clubs to play; we only wanted the odd trick to win the rubber,' said Rupert.

'But I hadn't another club to lead you,' exclaimed the Sheep, with his ready, defensive smile.

'It didn't occur to you to throw your queen away on my king and leave me with the command of the suit,' said Rupert, with polite bitterness.

'I suppose I ought to have – I wasn't certain what to do. I'm awfully sorry,' said the Sheep.

Being awfully and uselessly sorry formed a large part of his occupation in life. If a similar situation had arisen in a subsequent hand he would have blundered just as certainly, and he would have been just as irritatingly apologetic.

Rupert stared gloomily across at him as he sat smiling and fumbling with his cards. Many men who have good brains for business do not possess the rudiments of a card-brain, and Rupert would not have judged and condemned his prospective brother-in-law on the evidence of his bridge play alone. The tragic part of it was that he smiled and fumbled through life just as fatuously and apologetically as he did at the card-table. And behind the defensive smile and the well-worn expressions of regret there shone a scarcely believable but quite obvious self-satisfaction. Every sheep of the pasture probably imagines that in an emergency it could become terrible as an army with banners – one has only to watch how they stamp their feet and stiffen their necks when a minor object of suspicion comes into view and behaves meekly. And probably the majority of human sheep see themselves in imagination taking great parts in the world's more impressive dramas, forming swift, unerring decisions in moments of crisis, cowing mutinies, allaying panics, brave, strong, simple, but, in spite of their natural modesty, always slightly spectacular.

'Why in the name of all that is unnecessary and perverse should Kathleen choose this man for her future husband?' was the question that Rupert asked himself ruefully. There was young Malcolm Athling, as nice-looking, decent, level-headed a fellow as anyone could wish to meet, obviously her very devoted admirer, and yet she must throw herself away on this pale-eyed, weak-mouthed embodiment of self-approving ineptitude. If it had been merely Kathleen's own affair Rupert would have shrugged his shoulders and philosophically hoped that she might make the best of an undeniably bad bargain. But Rupert had no heir; his own boy lay underground somewhere on the Indian frontier, in goodly company. And the property would pass in due course to Kathleen and Kathleen's husband. The Sheep would live there in the beloved old home, rearing up other little Sheep, fatuous and rabbit-faced and self-satisfied like himself, to dwell in the land and possess it. It was not a soothing prospect.

Towards dusk on the afternoon following the bridge experience Rupert and the Sheep made their way homeward after a day's mixed shooting. The Sheep's cartridge bag was nearly empty, but his game bag showed no signs of overcrowding. The birds he had shot at had seemed for the most part as impervious to death or damage as the hero of a melodrama. And for each failure to drop his bird he had some explanation or apology ready on his lips. Now he was striding along in front of his host, chattering happily over his shoulder, but obviously on the look-out for some belated rabbit or wood-pigeon that might haply be secured as an eleventh hour addition to his bag. As they passed the edge of a small copse a large bird rose from the ground and flew slowly towards the trees, offering an easy shot to the oncoming sportsmen. The Sheep banged forth with both barrels, and gave an exultant cry.

'Hooray! I've shot a thundering big hawk.'

'To be exact, you've shot a honey-buzzard. That is the hen bird of one of the few pairs of honey-buzzards breeding in the United Kingdom. We've kept them under the strictest preservation for the last four years; every gamekeeper and village gun loafer for twenty miles round has been warned and bribed and threatened to respect their sanctity, and egg-snatching agents have been carefully guarded against during the breeding season. Hundreds of lovers of rare birds have delighted in seeing their snap-shotted portraits in *Country Life*, and now you've reduced the hen bird to a lump of broken feathers.'

Rupert spoke quietly and evenly, but for a moment or two a gleam of positive hatred shone in his eyes.

'I say, I'm so sorry,' said the Sheep, with his apologetic smile. 'Of course I remember hearing about the buzzards, but somehow I didn't connect this bird with them. And it was such an easy shot – '

'Yes,' said Rupert; 'that was the trouble.'

Kathleen found him in the gun-room smoothing out the feathers of the dead bird. She had already been told of the catastrophe.

'What a horrid misfortune,' she said sympathetically.

'It was my dear Robbie who first discovered them the last time he was home on leave. Don't you remember how excited he was about them? Let's go and have some tea.'

Both bridge and shooting were given a rest for the next two or three weeks. Death, who enters into no compacts with party whips, had forced a Parliamentary vacancy on the neighbourhood at the least convenient season, and the local partisans on either side found themselves immersed in the discomforts of a mid-winter election. Rupert took his politics seriously and keenly. He belonged to that type of strangely but rather happily constituted individual which these islands seem to produce in a fair plenty; men and women who for no personal profit or gain go forth from their comfortable firesides or club card-rooms to hunt to and fro in the mud and rain and wind for the capture or tracking of a stray vote here and there on their party's behalf – not because they think they ought to, but because they want to. And his energies were welcome enough on this occasion, for the seat was a closely disputed possession, and its loss or retention would count for much in the present position of the Parliamentary game. With Kathleen to help him, he had worked his corner of the constituency with tireless, well-directed zeal, taking his share of the dull routine work as well as of the livelier episodes. The talking part of the campaign wound up on the eve of the poll with a meeting in a centre where more undecided votes were supposed to be concentrated than anywhere else in the division. A good final meeting here would mean everything. And the speakers, local and imported, left nothing undone to improve the occasion. Rupert was down for the unimportant task of moving the complimentary vote to the chairman which should close the proceedings.

'I'm so hoarse,' he protested, when the moment arrived; 'I don't believe I can make my voice heard beyond the platform.'

'Let me do it,' said the Sheep; 'I'm rather good at that sort of thing.'

The chairman was popular with all parties, and the Sheep's opening words of complimentary recognition received a round of applause. The orator smiled expansively on his listeners and seized the opportunity to add a few words of political wisdom on his own account. People looked at the clock or began to grope for umbrellas and discarded neck-wraps. Then, in the midst of a string of meaningless platitudes, the Sheep delivered himself of one of those blundering remarks which travel from one end of a constituency to the other in half an hour, and are seized on by the other side as being more potent on their behalf than a ton of election literature. There was a general shuffling and muttering across the length and breadth of the hall, and a few hisses made themselves heard. The Sheep tried to whittle down his remark, and the chairman unhesitatingly threw him over in his speech of thanks, but the damage was done.

'I'm afraid I lost touch with the audience rather over that remark,' said the Sheep afterwards, with his apologetic smile abnormally developed.

'You lost us the election,' said the chairman, and he proved a true prophet.

A month or so of winter sport seemed a desirable pick-me-up after the strenuous work and crowning discomfiture of the election. Rupert and Kathleen hied them away to a small Alpine resort that was just coming into prominence, and thither the Sheep followed them in due course, in his rôle of husband-elect. The wedding had been fixed for the end of March.

It was a winter of early and unseasonable thaws, and the far end of the local lake, at a spot where swift currrents flowed into it, was decorated with notices written in three languages, warning skaters not to venture over certain unsafe patches. The folly of approaching too near these danger spots seemed to have a natural fascination for the Sheep.

'I don't see what possible danger there can be,' he protested, with his inevitable smile, when Rupert beckoned him away from the proscribed area; 'the milk that I put out on my window-sill last night was frozen an inch deep.'

'It hadn't got a strong current flowing through it,' said Rupert; 'in any case, there is not much sense in hovering round a doubtful piece of ice when there are acres of good ice to skate over. The secretary of the ice committee has warned you once already.'

A few minutes later Rupert heard a loud squeal of fear, and saw a dark spot blotting the smoothness of the lake's frozen surface. The Sheep was struggling helplessly in an ice-hole of his own making. Rupert gave one loud curse, and then dashed full tilt for the shore; outside a low stable building on the lake's edge he remembered having seen a ladder. If he could slide it across the ice-hole before the Sheep went under the rescue would be comparatively simple work. Other skaters were dashing up from a distance, and, with the ladder's help, they could get him out of his death-trap without having to trust themselves on the margin of rotten ice. Rupert sprang on to the surface of lumpy, frozen snow, and staggered to where the ladder lay. He had already lifted it when the rattle of a chain and a furious outburst of growls burst on his hearing, and he was dashed to the ground by a mass of white and tawny fur. A sturdy young yard-dog, frantic with the pleasure of performing his first piece of active guardian service, was ramping and snarling over him, rendering the task of regaining his feet or securing the ladder a matter of considerable difficulty. When he had at last succeeded in both efforts he was just by a hair's-breadth too late to be of any use. The Sheep had definitely disappeared under the ice-rift.

Kathleen Athling and her husband stay the greater part of the year with Rupert, and a small Robbie stands in some danger of being idolized by a devoted uncle. But for twelve months of the year Rupert's most inseparable and valued companion is a sturdy tawny and white yard-dog.

DISCONTENTED

Too Bad

'MY DEAR,' Mrs Marshall said to Mrs Ames, 'I never was so surprised in my life. Never in my life. Why, Grace and I were like that – just like *that*.'

She held up her right hand, the upstanding first and second fingers rigidly close together, in illustration.

Mrs Ames shook her head sadly, and offered the cinnamon toast.

'Imagine!' said Mrs Marshall, refusing it though with a longing eye. 'We were going to have dinner with them last Tuesday night, and then I got this letter from Grace from this little place up in Connecticut, saying she was going to be up there she didn't know how long, and she thought, when she came back, she'd probably take just one big room with a kitchenette. Ernest was living down at the club, she said.'

'But what did they do about their apartment?' Mrs Ames's voice was high with anxiety.

'Why, it seems his sister took it, furnished and all – by the way remind me, I must go and see her,' said Mrs Marshall. 'They wanted to move into town, anyway, and they were looking for a place.'

'Doesn't she feel terribly about it – his sister?' asked Mrs Ames.

'Oh – terribly.' Mrs Marshall dismissed the word as inadequate. 'My dear, think how everybody that knew them feels. Think how I feel. I don't know when I've had a thing depress me more. If it had been anybody but the Weldons!'

Mrs Ames nodded.

'That's what I said,' she reported.

'That's what everybody says.' Mrs Marshall quickly took away any undeserved credit. 'To think of the Weldons separating! Why,

I always used to say to Jim, "Well, there's one happily married couple, anyway," I used to say, "so congenial, and with that nice apartment, and all." And then, right out of a clear sky, they go and separate. I simply can't understand what on earth made them do it. It just seems too awful!'

Again Mrs Ames nodded, slowly and sadly.

'Yes, it always seems too bad, a thing like that does,' she said. 'It's too bad.'

II

Mrs Ernest Weldon wandered about the orderly living-room, giving it some of those little feminine touches. She was not especially good as a touch-giver. The idea was pretty, and appealing to her. Before she was married, she had dreamed of herself as moving softly about her new dwelling, deftly moving a vase here or straightening a flower there, and thus transforming it from a house to a home. Even now, after seven years of marriage, she liked to picture herself in the gracious act.

But, though she conscientiously made a try at it every night as soon as the rose-shaded lamps were lit, she was always a bit bewildered as to how one went about performing those tiny miracles that make all the difference in the world to a room. The living-room, it seemed to her, looked good enough as it was – as good as it would ever look, with that mantelpiece and the same old furniture. Delia, one of the most thoroughly feminine of creatures, had subjected it to a long series of emphatic touches earlier in the day, and none of her handiwork had since been disturbed. But the feat of making all the difference in the world, so Mrs Weldon had always heard, was not a thing to be left to servants. Touch-giving was a wife's job. And Mrs Weldon was not one to shirk the business she had entered.

With an almost pitiable air of uncertainty, she strayed over to the mantel, lifted a small Japanese vase, and stood with it in her hand, gazing helplessly around the room. The white-enamelled bookcase caught her eye, and gratefully she crossed to it and set the vase upon it, carefully rearranging various ornaments to make room. To relieve the congestion, she took up a framed photograph of Mr Weldon's sister in evening gown and eyeglasses, again looked all about, and then set it timidly on the piano. She smoothed the piano-cover ingratiatingly, straightened the copies of *A Day in Venice, To a Wild Rose,* and Kreisler's *Caprice Viennois,* which stood ever upon the rack, walked over to the tea-table and effected a change of places between the cream-jug and the sugar-bowl.

Then she stepped back, and surveyed her innovations. It was amazing how little difference they made to the room.

Sighing, Mrs Weldon turned her attention to a bowl of daffodils, slightly past their first freshness. There was nothing to be done there; the omniscient Delia had refreshed them with clear water, had clipped their stems, and removed their more passé sisters. Still Mrs Weldon bent over them pulling them gently about.

She liked to think of herself as one for whom flowers would thrive, who must always have blossoms about her, if she would be truly happy. When her living-room flowers died, she almost never forgot to stop in at the florist's the next day, and get a fresh bunch. She told people, in little bursts of confidence, that she loved flowers. There was something almost apologetic in her way of uttering her tender avowal, as if she would beg her listeners not to consider her too bizarre in her taste. It seemed rather as though she expected the hearer to fall back, startled, at her words, crying, 'Not really! Well, what *are* we coming to?'

She had other little confessions of affection, too, that she made from time to time; always with a little hesitation, as if understandably delicate about baring her heart, she told her love for colour, the country, a good time, a really interesting play, nice materials, well-made clothes, and sunshine. But it was her fondness for flowers that she acknowledged oftenest. She seemed to feel that this, even more than her other predilections, set her apart from the general.

Mrs Weldon gave the elderly daffodils a final pat, now, and once more surveyed the room, to see if any other repairs suggested themselves. Her lips tightened as the little Japanese vase met her gaze; distinctly, it had been better off in the first place. She set it back, the irritation that the sight of the mantel always gave her welling within her.

She had hated the mantelpiece from the moment they had first come to look at the apartment. There were other things that she had always hated about the place, too – the long, narrow hall, the dark dining-room, the inadequate closets. But Ernest had seemed to like the apartment well enough, so she had said nothing, then or since. After all, what was the use of fussing? Probably there would always be drawbacks, wherever they lived. There were enough in the last place they had had.

So they had taken the apartment on a five-year lease – there were four years and three months to go. Mrs Weldon felt suddenly weary. She lay down on the davenport, and pressed her thin hand against her dull brown hair.

Mr Weldon came down the street, bent almost double in his battle with the wind from the river. His mind went over its nightly dark thoughts on living near Riverside Drive, five blocks from a subway station – two of those blocks loud with savage gales. He did not much like their apartment, even when he reached it. As soon as he had seen that dining-room, he had realized that they must always breakfast by artificial light – a thing he hated. But Grace had never appeared to notice it, so he had held his peace. It didn't matter much, anyway, he explained to himself. There was pretty sure to be something wrong, everywhere. The dining-room wasn't much worse than that bedroom on the court, in the last place. Grace had never seemed to mind that, either.

Mrs Weldon opened the door at his ring.

'Well!' she said, cheerily.

They smiled brightly at each other.

'Hel-lo,' he said. 'Well! You home?'

They kissed, slightly. She watched with polite interest while he hung up his hat and coat, removed the evening papers from his pocket, and handed one to her.

'Bring the papers?' she said, taking it.

She preceded him along the narrow hall to the living-room, where he let himself slowly down into his big chair, with a sound between a sigh and a groan. She sat opposite him, on the davenport. Again they smiled brightly at each other.

'Well, what have you been doing with yourself today?' he inquired.

She had been expecting the question. She had planned before he came in, how she would tell him all the little events of her day – how the woman in the grocer's shop had had an argument with the cashier, and how Delia had tried out a new salad for lunch with but moderate success, and how Alice Marshall had come to tea and it was quite true that Norma Matthews was going to have another baby. She had woven them into a lively little narrative, carefully choosing amusing phrases of description; had felt that she was going to tell it well and with spirit, and that he might laugh at the account of the occurrence in the grocer's. But now, as she considered it, it seemed to her a long, dull story. She had not the energy to begin it. And he was already smoothing out his paper.

'Oh, nothing,' she said, with a gay little laugh. 'Did you have a nice day?'

'Why – ' he began. He had had some idea of telling her how he had finally put through that Detroit thing, and how tickled J.G. had seemed to be about it. But his interest waned, even as he started to speak. Besides, she was engrossed in breaking off a loose thread from the wool fringe on one of the pillows beside her.

'Oh, pretty fair,' he said.

'Tired?' she asked.

'Not so much,' he answered. 'Why – want to do anything tonight?'

'Why, not unless you do,' she said, brightly. 'Whatever you say.'

'Whatever *you* say,' he corrected her.

The subject closed. There was a third exchange of smiles, and then he hid most of himself behind his paper.

Mrs Weldon, too, turned to the newspaper. But it was an off night for news – a long speech of somebody's, a plan for a garbage dump, a proposed dirigible, a four-day-old murder mystery. No one she knew had died or become engaged or married, or had attended any social functions. The fashions depicted on the woman's page were for Miss Fourteen-to-Sixteen. The advertisements ran mostly to bread, and sauces, and men's clothes and sales of kitchen utensils. She put the paper down.

She wondered how Ernest could get so much enjoyment out of a newspaper. He could occupy himself with one for almost an hour, and then pick up another and go all through the same news with unabated interest. She wished that she could. She wished, even more than that, that she could think of something to say. She glanced around the room for inspiration.

'See my pretty daffy-down-dillies?' she said, finding it. To anyone else, she would have referred to them as daffodils.

Mr Weldon looked in the direction of the flowers.

'M-m-mm,' he said in admission, and returned to the news.

She looked at him, and shook her head despondently. He did not see, behind the paper; nor did she see that he was not reading. He was waiting, his hands gripping the printed sheet till their knuckles were blue-white, for her next remark.

It came.

'I love flowers,' she said, in one of her little rushes of confidence.

Her husband did not answer. He sighed, his grip relaxed, and he went on reading.

Mrs Weldon searched the room for another suggestion.

'Ernie,' she said, 'I'm so comfortable. Wouldn't you like to get up and get my handkerchief off the piano for me?'

He rose instantly. 'Why, certainly,' he said.

The way to ask people to fetch handkerchiefs, he thought as

he went back to his chair, was to ask them to do it, and not try to make them think that you were giving them a treat. Either come right out and ask them, would they or wouldn't they, or else get up and get your handkerchief yourself.

'Thank you ever so much,' his wife said with enthusiasm.

Delia appeared in the doorway. 'Dinner,' she murmured bashfully, as if it were not quite a nice word for a young woman to use, and vanished.

'Dinner, Ern,' cried Mrs Weldon gaily, getting up.

'Just a minute,' issued indistinctly from behind the newspaper.

Mrs Weldon waited. Then her lips compressed, and she went over and playfully took the paper from her husband's hands. She smiled carefully at him, and he smiled back at her.

'You go ahead in,' he said, rising. 'I'll be right with you. I've just got to wash up.'

She looked after him, and something like a volcanic eruption took place within her. You'd think that just one night – just one little night – he might go and wash before dinner was announced. Just one night – it didn't seem much to ask. But she said nothing. God knew it was aggravating, but after all, it wasn't worth the trouble of fussing about.

She was waiting, cheerful and bright, courteously refraining from beginning her soup, when he took his place at the table.

'Oh, tomato soup, eh?' he said.

'Yes,' she answered. 'You like it, don't you?'

'Who – me?' he said. 'Oh, yes. Yes, indeed.'

She smiled at him.

'Yes, I thought you liked it,' she said.

'You like it, too, don't you?' he inquired.

'Oh, yes,' she assured him. 'Yes, I like it ever so much. I'm awfully fond of tomato soup.'

'Yes,' he said, 'there's nothing much better than tomato soup on a cold night.'

She nodded.

'I think it's nice, too,' she confided.

They had had tomato soup for dinner probably three times a month during their married life.

The soup was finished, and Delia brought in the meat.

'Well, that looks pretty good,' said Mr Weldon, carving it. 'We haven't had steak for a long time.'

'Why, yes, we have, too, Ern,' his wife said eagerly. 'We had it – let me see, what night were the Baileys here? – we had it Wednesday night – no, Thursday night. Don't you remember?'

'Did we?' he said. 'Yes, I guess you're right. It seemed longer, somehow.'

Mrs Weldon smiled politely. She could not think of any way to prolong the discussion.

What did married people talk about, anyway, when they were alone together? She had seen married couples – not dubious ones but people she really knew were husbands and wives – at the theatre or in trains, talking together as animatedly as if they were just acquaintances. She always watched them, marvellingly, wondering what on earth they found to say.

She could talk well enough to other people. There never seemed to be enough time for her to finish saying all she wanted to to her friends; she recalled how she had run on to Alice Marshall, only that afternoon. Both men and women found her attractive to listen to; not brilliant, not particularly funny, but still amusing and agreeable. She was never at a loss for something to say, never conscious of groping around for a topic. She had a good memory for bits of fresh gossip, or little stories of some celebrity that she had read or heard somewhere, and a knack of telling them entertainingly. Things people said to her stimulated her to quick replies, and more amusing narratives. They weren't especially scintillating people, either; it was just that they talked to her.

That was the trick of it. If nobody said anything to you, how were you to carry on a conversation from there? Inside, she was always bitter and angry at Ernest for not helping her out.

Ernest, too, seemed to be talkative enough when he was with others. People were always coming up and telling her how much they had enjoyed meeting her husband, and what fun he was. They weren't just being polite. There was no reason why they should go out of their way to say it.

Even when she and Ernest had another couple in to dinner or bridge, they both talked and laughed easily, all evening long. But as soon as the guests said good night and what an awfully nice evening it had been, and the door had closed behind them, there the Weldons were again, without a word to say to each other. It would have been intimate and amusing to have talked over their guests' clothes and skill at bridge and probable domestic and financial affairs, and she would do it the next day, with great interest, too, to Alice Marshall, or some other one of her friends. But she couldn't do it with Ernest. Just as she started to, she found she simply couldn't make the effort.

So they would put away the card-table and empty the ash-receivers, with many 'Oh, I beg your pardon's and 'No, no – I was in your way's, and then Ernest would say, 'Well, I guess I'll go along to bed,' and she would answer, 'All right – I'll be in in a minute,' and they would smile cheerfully at each other, and another evening would be over.

She tried to remember what they used to talk about before they were married, when they were engaged. It seemed to her that they never had had much to say to each other. But she hadn't worried about it then; indeed, she had felt the satisfaction of the correct, in their courtship, for she had always heard that true love was inarticulate. Then, besides, there had been always kissing and things, to take up your mind. But it had turned out that true marriage was apparently equally dumb. And you can't depend on kisses and all the rest of it to while away the evenings, after seven years.

You'd think that you would get used to it, in seven years, would realize that that was the way it was, and let it go at that. You don't, though. A thing like that gets on your nerves. It isn't one of those cozy, companionable silences that people occasionally fall into together. It makes you feel as if you must do something about it, as if you weren't performing your duty. You have the feeling a hostess has when her party is going badly, when her guests sit in corners and refuse to mingle. It makes you nervous and self-conscious, and you talk desperately about tomato soup, and say things like 'daffy-down-dilly'.

Mrs Weldon cast about in her mind for a subject to offer her husband. There was Alice Marshall's new system of reducing – no, that was pretty dull. There was the case she had read in the morning's paper about the man of eighty-seven who had taken, as his fourth wife, a girl of twenty – he had probably seen that, and as long as he hadn't thought it worth repeating, he wouldn't think it worth hearing. There was the thing the Baileys' little boy had said about Jesus – no, she had told him that the night before.

She looked over at him, desultorily eating his rhubarb pie. She wished he wouldn't put that greasy stuff on his head. Perhaps it was necessary, if his hair really was falling out, but it did seem that he might find some more attractive remedy, if he only had the consideration to look around for one. Anyway, why must his hair fall out? There was something a little disgusting about people with falling hair.

'Like your pie, Ernie?' she asked vivaciously.

'Why, I don't know,' he said, thinking it over. 'I'm not so crazy about rhubarb, I don't think. Are you?'

'No, I'm not so awfully crazy about it,' she answered. 'But, then, I'm not really crazy about any kind of pie.'

'Aren't you really?' he said, politely surprised. 'I like pie pretty well – some kinds of pie.'

'Do you?' The polite surprise was hers now.

'Why, yes,' he said. 'I like a nice huckleberry pie, or a nice lemon meringue pie, or a – ' He lost interest in the thing himself, and his voice died away.

He avoided looking at her left hand, which lay on the edge of the table, palm upward. The long, grey-white ends of her nails protruded beyond the tips of her fingers, and the sight made him uncomfortable. Why in God's name must she wear her finger nails that preposterous length, and file them to those horrible points? If there was anything that he hated, it was a woman with pointed finger nails.

They returned to the living-room, and Mr Weldon again eased himself down into his chair, reaching for the second paper.

'Quite sure there isn't anything you'd like to do tonight?' he asked solicitously. 'Like to go to the movies, or anything?'

'Oh, no,' she said. 'Unless there's something you want to do.'

'No, no,' he answered. 'I just thought maybe you wanted to.'

'Not unless you do,' she said.

He began on his paper, and she wandered aimlessly about the room. She had forgotten to get a new book from the library, and it had never in her life occurred to her to re-read a book that she had once completed. She thought vaguely of playing solitaire, but she did not care enough about it to go to the trouble of getting out the cards, and setting up the table. There was some sewing that she could do, and she thought that she might presently go into the bedroom and fetch the nightgown that she was making for herself. Yes, she would probably do that, in a little while.

Ernest would read industriously, and, along toward the middle of the paper, he would start yawning aloud. Something happened inside Mrs Weldon when he did this. She would murmur that she had to speak to Delia, and hurry to the kitchen. She would stay there rather a long time, looking vaguely into jars and inquiring half-heartedly about laundry lists, and, when she returned, he would have gone in to get ready for bed.

In a year, three hundred of their evenings were like this. Seven times three hundred is more than two thousand.

Mrs Weldon went into the bedroom, and brought back her sewing. She sat down, pinned the pink satin to her knee, and began whipping narrow lace along the top of the half-made garment. It was fussy work. The fine thread knotted and drew, and she could not get the light adjusted so that the shadow of her head did not fall on her work. She grew a little sick, from the strain on her eyes.

Mr Weldon turned a page, and yawned aloud. 'Wah-huh-huh-huh-huh,' he went, on a descending scale. He yawned again, and this time climbed the scale.

III

'My dear,' Mrs Ames said to Mrs Marshall, 'don't you really think that there must have been some other woman?'

'Oh, I simply couldn't think it was anything like that,' said Mrs Marshall. 'Not Ernest Weldon. So devoted – home every night at half-past six, and such good company, and so jolly, and all. I don't see how there *could* have been.'

'Sometimes,' observed Mrs Ames, 'those awfully jolly men at home are just the kind.'

'Yes, I know,' Mrs Marshall said. 'But not Ernest Weldon. Why, I used to say to Jim, "I never saw such a devoted husband in my life," I said. Oh, not Ernest Weldon.'

'I don't suppose,' began Mrs Ames, and hesitated. 'I don't suppose,' she went on, intently pressing the bit of sodden lemon in her cup with her teaspoon, 'that Grace – that there was ever anyone – or anything like that?'

'Oh, heavens, no,' cried Mrs Marshall. 'Grace Weldon just gave her whole life to that man. It was Ernest this and Ernest that every minute. I simply can't understand it. If there was one earthly reason – if they ever fought, or if Ernest drank, or anything like that. But they got along so beautifully together – why, it just seems as if they must have been crazy to go and do a thing like this. Well, I can't begin to tell you how blue it's made me. It seems so awful!'

'Yes,' said Mrs Ames, 'it certainly is too bad.'

The Mappined Life

'THESE Mappin Terraces at the Zoological Gardens are a great improvement on the old style of wild-beast cage,' said Mrs James Gurtleberry, putting down an illustrated paper; 'they give one the illusion of seeing the animals in their natural surroundings. I wonder how much of the illusion is passed on to the animals?'

'That would depend on the animal,' said her niece; 'a jungle-fowl, for instance, would no doubt think its lawful jungle surrounding were faithfully reproduced if you gave it a sufficiency of wives, a goodly variety of seed food and ants' eggs, a commodious bank of loose earth to dust itself in, a convenient roosting tree, and a rival or two to make matters interesting. Of course there ought to be jungle-cats and birds of prey and other agencies of sudden death to add to the illusion of liberty, but the bird's own imagination is capable of inventing those – look how a domestic fowl will squawk an alarm note if a rook or wood-pigeon passes over its run when it has chickens.'

'You think, then, they really do have a sort of illusion, if you give them space enough – '

'In a few cases only. Nothing will make me believe that an acre or so of concrete enclosure will make up to a wolf or a tiger-cat for the range of night prowling that would belong to it in a wild state. Think of the dictionary of sound and scent and recollection that unfolds before a real wild beast as it comes out from its lair every evening, with the knowledge that in a few minutes it will be hieing along to some distant hunting ground where all the joy and fury of the chase awaits it; think of the crowded sensations of the brain when every rustle, every cry, every bent twig, and every whiff across the nostrils means something, something to do with life and death and dinner. Imagine the satisfaction of stealing down to your own particular drinking spot, choosing your own particular tree to scrape your claws on, finding your own particular bed of dried grass to roll on. Then, in the place of all that, put a concrete promenade, which will be of exactly the same dimensions whether you race or crawl across it, coated with stale, unvarying scents and surrounded with cries and noises that have ceased to have the least meaning or interest. As a substitute for a narrow cage the new enclosures are excellent, but I should think they are a poor imitation of a life of liberty.'

'It's rather depressing to think that,' said Mrs Gurtleberry; 'they look so spacious and so natural, but I suppose a good deal of what seems natural to us would be meaningless to a wild animal.'

'That is where our superior powers of self-deception come in,' said the niece; 'we are able to live our unreal, stupid little lives on our particular Mappin terrace, and persuade ourselves that we really are untrammelled men and women leading a reasonable existence in a reasonable sphere.'

'But good gracious,' exclaimed the aunt, bouncing into an attitude of scandalized defence, 'we are leading reasonable existences! What on earth do you mean by trammels? We are merely trammelled by the ordinary decent conventions of civilized society.'

'We are trammelled,' said the niece, calmly and pitilessly, 'by restrictions of income and opportunity, and above all by lack of initiative. To some people a restricted income doesn't matter a bit, in fact it often seems to help as a means for getting a lot of reality out of life; I am sure there are men and women who do their shopping in little back streets of Paris, buying four carrots and a shred of beef for their daily sustenance, who lead a perfectly real and eventful existence. Lack of initiative is the thing that really cripples one, and that is where you and I and Uncle James are so hopelessly shut in. We are just so many animals stuck down on a Mappin terrace, with this difference in our disfavour, that the animals are there to be looked at, while nobody wants to look at us. As a matter of fact there would be nothing to look at. We get colds in winter and hay-fever in summer, and if a wasp happens to sting one of us, well, that is the wasp's initiative, not ours; all we do is to wait for the swelling to go down. Whenever we do climb into local fame and notice, it is by indirect methods; if it happens to be a good flowering year for magnolias the neighbourhood observes, "Have you seen the Gurtleberrys' magnolia? It is a perfect mass of flowers," and we go about telling people that there are fifty-seven blossoms as against thirty-nine the previous year.'

'In Coronation year there were as many as sixty,' put in the aunt; 'your uncle has kept a record for the last eight years.'

'Doesn't it ever strike you,' continued the niece relentlessly, 'that if we moved away from here or were blotted out of existence our local claim to fame would pass automatically to whoever happened to take the house and garden? People would say to one another, "Have you seen the Smith-Jenkins' magnolia? It is a perfect mass of flowers," or else, "Smith-Jenkins tells me there won't be a single blossom on their magnolia this year; the east winds have turned all the buds black." Now if, when we had gone, people still associated our names with the magnolia tree, no matter who temporarily possessed it, if they said, "Ah, that's the tree on which the Gurtleberrys hung their cook because she sent up the wrong kind of sauce with the asparagus," that would be something really due to our own initiative, apart from anything east winds or magnolia vitality might have to say in the matter.'

'We should never do such a thing,' said the aunt. The niece gave a reluctant sigh.

'I can't imagine it,' she admitted. 'Of course,' she continued, 'there are heaps of ways of leading a real existence without committing sensational deeds of violence. It's the dreadful little everyday acts of pretended importance that give the Mappin stamp to our life. It would be entertaining, if it wasn't so pathetically tragic, to hear Uncle James fuss in here in the morning and announce, "I must just go down into the town and find out what the men there are saying about Mexico. Matters are beginning to look serious there." Then he patters away into the town, and talks in a highly serious voice to the tobacconist, incidentally buying an ounce of tobacco; perhaps he meets one or two others of the world's thinkers and talks to them in a highly serious voice, then he patters back here and announces with increased importance, "I've just been talking to some men in the town about the conditions of affairs in Mexico. They agree with the view that I have formed, that things there will have to get worse before they get better." Of course nobody in the town cared in the least little bit what his views about Mexico were or whether he had any. The tobacconist wasn't even fluttered at his buying the ounce of tobacco; he knows that he purchases the same quantity of the same sort of tobacco every week. Uncle James might just as well have lain on his back in the garden and chattered to the lilac tree about the habits of caterpillars.'

'I really will not listen to such things about your uncle,' protested Mrs James Gurtleberry angrily.

'My own case is just as bad and just as tragic,' said the niece dispassionately; 'nearly everything about me is conventional make-believe. I'm not a good dancer, and no one could honestly call me good-looking, but when I go to one of our dull little local dances I'm conventionally supposed to "have a heavenly time", to attract the ardent homage of the local cavaliers, and to go home with my head awhirl with pleasurable recollections. As a matter of fact, I've merely put in some hours of indifferent dancing, drunk some badly made claret cup, and listened to an enormous amount of laborious light conversation. A moonlight hen-stealing raid with the merry-eyed curate could be infinitely more exciting; imagine the pleasure of carrying off all those white Minorcas that the Chibfords are always bragging about. When we had disposed of them we could give the proceeds to a charity, so there would be nothing really wrong about it. But nothing of that sort lies within the Mappined limits of my life. One of these days somebody dull and decorous and undistinguished will "make himself agreeable" to me at a tennis party, as the saying is, and all the dull old gossips of the neighbourhood will begin to ask when we are to be engaged, and at last we shall be engaged, and people will give us butter-dishes and blotting-cases, and framed pictures of young women feeding swans. Hullo, Uncle, are you going out?'

'I'm just going down to the town,' announced Mr James Gurtleberry, with an air of some importance: 'I want to hear what people are saying about Albania. Affairs there are beginning to take on a very serious look. It's my opinion that we haven't seen the worst of things yet.'

In this he was probably right, but there was nothing in the immediate or prospective condition of Albania to warrant Mrs Gurtleberry in bursting into tears.

The Philanthropist and the Happy Cat

JOCANTHA BESSBURY was in the mood to be serenely and graciously happy. Her world was a pleasant place, and it was wearing one of its pleasantest aspects. Gregory had managed to get home for a hurried lunch and a smoke afterwards in the little snuggery; the lunch had been a good one, and there was just time to do justice to the coffee and cigarettes. Both were excellent in their way, and Gregory was, in his way, an excellent husband. Jocantha rather suspected herself of making him a very charming wife, and more than suspected herself of having a first-rate dressmaker.

'I don't suppose a more thoroughly contented personality is to be found in all Chelsea,' observed Jocantha in allusion to herself; 'except perhaps Attab,' she continued, glancing towards the large tabby-marked cat that lay in considerable ease in a corner of the divan. 'He lies there, purring and dreaming, shifting his limbs now and then in an ecstasy of cushioned comfort. He seems the incarnation of everything soft and silky and velvety, without a sharp edge in his composition, a dreamer whose philosophy is sleep and let sleep; and then, as evening draws on, he goes out into the garden with a red glint in his eyes and slays a drowsy sparrow.'

'As every pair of sparrows hatches out ten or more young ones in the year, while their food supply remains stationary, it is just as well that the Attabs of the community should have that idea of how to pass an amusing afternoon,' said Gregory. Having delivered himself of this sage comment he lit another cigarette, bade Jocantha a playfully affectionate good-bye, and departed into the outer world.

'Remember, dinner's a wee bit earlier tonight, as we're going to the Haymarket,' she called after him.

Left to herself, Jocantha continued the process of looking at her life with placid, introspective eyes. If she had not everything she wanted in this world, at least she was very well pleased with what she had got. She was very well pleased, for instance, with the snuggery, which contrived somehow to be cosy and dainty and expensive all at once. The porcelain was rare and beautiful, the Chinese enamels took on wonderful tints in the firelight, the rugs and hangings led the eye through sumptuous harmonies of colouring. It was a room in which one might have suitably entertained an ambassador or an archbishop, but it was also a room in which one could cut out pictures for a scrap-book without feeling that one was scandalizing the deities of the place with one's litter. And as with the snuggery, so with the rest of the house, and as with the house, so with the other departments of Jocantha's life; she really had good reason for being one of the most contented women in Chelsea.

From being in a mood of simmering satisfaction with her lot she passed to the phase of being generously commiserating for those thousands around her whose lives and circumstances were dull, cheap, pleasureless, and empty. Work girls, shop assistants and so forth, the class that have neither the happy-go-lucky freedom of the poor nor the leisured freedom of the rich, came specially within the range of her sympathy. It was sad to think that there were young people who, after a long day's work, had to sit alone in chill, dreary bedrooms because they could not afford the price of a cup of coffee and a sandwich in a restaurant, still less a shilling for a theatre gallery.

Jocantha's mind was still dwelling on this theme when she started forth on an afternoon campaign of desultory shopping; it would be rather a comforting thing, she told herself, if she could do something, on the spur of the moment, to bring a gleam of pleasure and interest into the life of even one or two wistful-hearted, empty-pocketed workers; it would add a good deal to her sense of enjoyment at the theatre that night. She would get two upper circle tickets for a popular play, make her way into some cheap tea-shop, and present the tickets to the first couple of interesting work girls with whom she could casually drop into conversation. She could explain matters by saying that she was unable to use the tickets herself and did not want them to be wasted, and, on the other hand, did not want the trouble of sending them back. On further reflection she decided that it might be better to get only one ticket and give it to some lonely-looking girl sitting eating her frugal meal by herself; the girl might scrape acquaintance with her next-seat neighbour at the theatre and lay the foundations of a lasting friendship.

With the Fairy Godmother impulse strong upon her, Jocantha marched into a ticket agency and selected with immense care an upper circle seat for the 'Yellow Peacock', a play that was attracting a considerable amount of discussion and criticism. Then she went forth in search of a tea-shop and philanthropic adventure, at about the same time that Attab sauntered into the garden with a mind attuned to sparrow stalking. In a corner of an A.B.C. shop she found an unoccupied table, whereat she promptly installed herself, impelled by the fact that at the next table was sitting a young girl, rather plain of feature, with tired, listless eyes and a general air of uncomplaining forlornness. Her dress was of poor material, but aimed at being in the fashion, her hair was pretty, and her complexion bad; she was finishing a modest meal of tea and scone, and she was not very different in her way from thousands of other girls who were finishing, or beginning, or continuing their teas in London tea-shops at that exact moment. The odds were enormously in favour of the supposition that she had never seen the 'Yellow Peacock'; obviously she supplied excellent material for Jocantha's first experiment in haphazard benefaction.

Jocantha ordered some tea and a muffin, and then turned a friendly scrutiny on her neighbour with a view to catching her eye. At that precise moment the girl's face lit up with sudden pleasure, her eyes sparkled, a flush came into her cheeks, and she looked almost pretty. A young man, whom she greeted with an effectionate

'Hullo, Bertie' came up to her table and took his seat in a chair facing her. Jocantha looked hard at the new-comer; he was in appearance a few years younger than herself, very much better-looking than Gregory, rather better-looking, in fact, than any of the young men of her set. She guessed him to be a well-mannered young clerk in some wholesale warehouse, existing and amusing himself as best he might on a tiny salary, and commanding a holiday of about two weeks in the year. He was aware, of course, of his good looks, but with the shy self-consciousness of the Anglo-Saxon, not the blatant complacency of the Latin or Semite. He was obviously on terms of friendly intimacy with the girl he was talking to, probably they were drifting towards a formal engagement. Jocantha pictured the boy's home, in a rather narrow circle, with a tiresome mother who always wanted to know how and where he spent his evenings. He would exchange that humdrum thraldom in due course for a home of his own, dominated by a chronic scarcity of pounds, shillings, and pence, and a dearth of most of the things that made life attractive or comfortable. Jocantha felt extremely sorry for him. She wondered if he had seen the 'Yellow Peacock'; the odds were enormously in favour of the supposition that he had not. The girl had finished her tea, and would shortly be going back to her work; when the boy was alone it would be quite easy for Jocantha to say: 'My husband has made other arrangements for me this evening; would you care to make use of this ticket, which would otherwise be wasted?' Then she could come there again one afternoon for tea, and, if she saw him, ask him how he liked the play. If he was a nice boy and improved on acquaintance he could be given more theatre tickets and perhaps asked to come one Sunday to tea at Chelsea. Jocantha made up her mind that he would improve on acquaintance, and that Gregory would like him, and that the Fairy Godmother business would prove far more entertaining than she had originally anticipated. The boy was distinctly presentable; he knew how to brush his hair, which was possibly an imitative faculty; he knew what colour of tie suited him, which might be intuition; he was exactly the type that Jocantha admired, which of course was accident. Altogether she was rather pleased when the girl looked at the clock and bade a friendly but unhurried farewell to her companion. Bertie nodded 'good-bye', gulped down a mouthful of tea, and then produced from his overcoat pocket a paper-covered book, bearing the title *Sepoy and Sahib, a Tale of the Great Mutiny*.

The laws of tea-shop etiquette forbid that you should offer theatre tickets to a stranger without having first caught the stranger's eye. It is even better if you can ask to have a sugar basin passed to you, having previously concealed the fact that you have a large and well-filled sugar basin on your own table; this is not difficult to manage, as the printed menu is generally nearly as large as the table, and can be made to stand on end. Jocantha set to work hopefully; she had a long and rather high-pitched discussion with the waitress concerning alleged defects in an altogether blameless muffin, she made loud and plaintive inquiries about the tube service to some impossibly remote suburb, she talked with brilliant insincerity to the tea-shop kitten, and as a last resort she upset a milk-jug and swore at it daintily. Altogether she attracted a good deal of attention, but never for a moment did she attract the attention of the boy with the beautifully brushed hair, who was some thousands of miles away in the baking plains of Hindostan, amid deserted bungalows, seething bazaars, and riotous barracks squares, listening to the throbbing of tom-toms and the distant rattle of musketry.

Jocantha went back to her house in Chelsea, which struck her for the first time as looking dull and over-furnished. She had a resentful conviction that Gregory would be uninteresting at dinner, and that the play would be stupid after dinner. On the whole her frame of mind showed a marked divergence from the purring complacency of Attab, who was again curled up in his corner of the divan with a great peace radiating from every curve of his body.

But then he had killed his sparrow.

MARRIED LIFE

Here We Are

THE young man in the new blue suit finished arranging the glistening luggage in tight corners of the Pullman compartment. The train had leaped at curves and bounced along straight-aways, rendering balance a praiseworthy achievement and a sporadic one; and the young man had pushed and hoisted and tucked and shifted the bags with concentrated care.

Nevertheless, eight minutes for the settling of two suitcases and a hat-box is a long time.

He sat down, leaning back against bristled green plush, in the seat opposite the girl in beige. She looked as new as a peeled egg. Her hat, her fur, her frock, her gloves were glossy and stiff with novelty. On the arc of the thin, slippery sole of one beige shoe was gummed a tiny oblong of white paper, printed with the price set and paid for that slipper and its fellow, and the name of the shop that had dispensed them.

She had been staring raptly out of the window, drinking in the big weathered signboards that extolled the phenomena of codfish without bones and screens no rust could corrrupt. As the young man sat down, she turned politely from the pane, met his eyes, started a smile and got it about half done, and rested her gaze just above his right shoulder.

'Well!' the young man said.

'Well!' she said.

'Well, here we are,' he said.

'Here we are,' she said. 'Aren't we?'

'I should say we were,' he said. 'Eeyop. Here we are.'

'Well!' she said.

'Well!' he said. 'Well. How does it feel to be an old married lady?'

'Oh, it's too soon to ask me that,' she said. 'At least – I mean. Well, I mean, goodness, we've only been married about three hours, haven't we?'

The young man studied his wrist-watch as if he were just acquiring the knack of reading time.

'We have been married,' he said, 'exactly two hours and twenty-six minutes.'

'My,' she said. 'It seems like longer.'

'No,' he said. 'It isn't hardly half-past six yet.'

'It seems like later,' she said. 'I guess it's because it starts getting dark so early.'

'It does, at that,' he said. 'The nights are going to be pretty long from now on. I mean. I mean – well, it starts getting dark early.'

'I didn't have any idea what time it was,' she said. 'Everything was so mixed up, I sort of don't know where I am, or what it's all about. Getting back from the church, and then all those people, and then changing all my clothes, and then everybody throwing things, and all. Goodness, I don't see how people do it every day.'

'Do what?' he said.

'Get married,' she said. 'When you think of all the people, all over the world, getting married just as if it was nothing. Chinese people and everybody. Just as if it wasn't anything.'

'Well, let's not worry about people all over the world,' he said. 'Let's don't think about a lot of Chinese. We've got something better to think about. I mean. I mean – well, what do we care about them?'

'I know,' she said. 'But I just sort of got to thinking of them, all of them, all over everywhere, doing it all the time. At least, I mean – getting married, you know. And it's – well, it's sort of such a big thing to do, it makes you feel queer. You think of them, all of them, all doing it just like it wasn't anything. And how does anybody know what's going to happen next?'

'Let them worry,' he said. 'We don't have to. We know darn well what's going to happen next. I mean. I mean – well, we know it's going to be great. Well, we know we're going to be happy. Don't we?'

'Oh, of course,' she said. 'Only you think of all the people, and you have to sort of keep thinking. It makes you feel funny. An awful lot of people that get married, it doesn't turn out so well. And I guess they all must have thought it was going to be great.'

'Come on, now,' he said. 'This is no way to start a honeymoon, with all this thinking going on. Look at us – all married and everything done. I mean. The wedding all done and all.'

'Ah, it was nice, wasn't it?' she said. 'Did you really like my veil?'

'You looked great,' he said. 'Just great.'

'Oh, I'm terribly glad,' she said. 'Ellie and Louise looked lovely, didn't they? I'm terribly glad they did finally decide on pink. They looked perfectly lovely.'

'Listen,' he said. 'I want to tell you something. When I was standing up there in that old church waiting for you to come up, and I saw those two bridesmaids, I thought to myself, I thought, "Well, I never knew Louise could look like that!" Why, she'd have knocked anybody's eye out.'

'Oh, really?' she said. 'Funny. Of course, everybody thought her dress and hat were lovely, but a lot of people seemed to think she looked sort of tired. People have been saying that a lot, lately. I tell them I think it's awfully mean of them to go around saying that about her. I tell them they've got to remember that Louise isn't so terribly young any more, and they've got to expect her to look like that. Louise can say she's twenty-three all she wants to, but she's a good deal nearer twenty-seven.'

'Well, she was certainly a knock-out at the wedding,' he said. 'Boy!'

'I'm terribly glad you thought so,' she said. 'I'm glad someone did. How did you think Ellie looked?'

'Why, I honestly didn't get a look at her,' he said.

'Oh, really?' she said. 'Well, I certainly think that's too bad. I don't suppose I ought to say it about my own sister, but I never saw anybody look as beautiful as Ellie looked today. And always so sweet and unselfish, too. And you didn't even notice her. But you never pay attention to Ellie, anyway. Don't think I haven't noticed it. It makes me feel just terrible. It makes me feel just awful, that you don't like my own sister.'

'I do so like her!' he said. 'I'm crazy for Ellie. I think she's a great kid.'

'Don't think it makes any difference to Ellie!' she said. 'Ellie's got enough people crazy about her. It isn't anything to her whether you like her or not. Don't flatter yourself she cares! Only, the only thing is, it makes it awfully hard for me you don't like her, that's the only thing. I keep thinking, when we come back and get in the apartment and everything, it's going to be awfully hard for me that you won't want my own sister to come and see me. It's going to make it awfully hard for me that you won't ever want my family around. I know how you feel about my family. Don't think I haven't seen it. Only, if you don't ever want to see them, that's your loss. Not theirs. Don't flatter yourself!'

'Oh, now, come on!' he said. 'What's all this talk about not wanting your family around? Why, you know how I feel about your family. I think your old lady – I think your mother's swell. And Ellie. And your father. What's all this talk?'

'Well, I've seen it,' she said. 'Don't think I haven't. Lots of people they get married, and they think it's going to be great and everything, and then it all goes to pieces because people don't like people's families, or something like that. Don't tell me! I've seen it happen.'

'Honey,' he said, 'what is all this? What are you getting all angry about? Hey, look, this is our honeymoon. What are you trying to start a fight for? Ah, I guess you're just feeling sort of nervous.'

'Me?' she said. 'What have I got to be nervous about? I mean. I mean, goodness, I'm not nervous.'

'You know, lots of times,' he said, 'they say that girls get kind of nervous and yippy on account of thinking about – I mean. I mean – well, it's like you said, things are all so sort of mixed up and everything, right now. But afterwards, it'll be all right. I mean. I mean – well, look, honey, you don't look any too comfortable. Don't you want to take your hat off? And let's don't ever fight, ever. Will we?'

'Ah, I'm sorry I was cross,' she said. 'I guess I did feel a little bit funny. All mixed up, and then thinking of all those people all over everywhere, and then being sort of 'way off here, all alone with you. It's so sort of different. It's sort of such a big thing. You can't blame a person for thinking, can you? Yes, don't let's ever, ever fight. We won't be like a whole lot of them. We won't fight or be nasty or anything. Will we?'

'You bet your life we won't,' he said.

'I guess I will take this darned old hat off,' she said. 'It kind of presses. Just put it up on the rack, will you, dear? Do you like it, sweetheart?'

'Looks good on you,' he said.

'No, but I mean,' she said, 'do you really like it?'

'Well, I'll tell you,' he said. 'I know this is the new style and everything like that, and it's probably great. I don't know anything about things like that. Only I like the kind of a hat like that blue hat you had. Gee, I liked that hat.'

'Oh, really?' she said. 'Well, that's nice. That's lovely. The first thing you say to me, as soon as you get me off on a train away from my family and everything, is that you don't like my hat. The first thing you say to your wife is you think she has terrible taste in hats. That's nice, isn't it?'

'Now, honey,' he said, 'I never said anything like that. I only said—'

'What you don't seem to realize,' she said, 'is this hat cost twenty-two dollars. Twenty-two dollars. And that horrible old blue thing you think you're so crazy about, that cost three ninety-five.'

'I don't give a darn what they cost,' he said. 'I only said – I said I liked that blue hat. I don't know anything about hats. I'll be crazy about this one as soon as I get used to it. Only it's kind of not like your other hats. I don't know about the new styles. What do I know about women's hats?'

'It's too bad,' she said, 'you didn't marry somebody that would get the kind of hats you'd like. Hat's that cost three ninety-five. Why didn't you marry Louise? You always think she looks so beautiful. You'd love her taste in hats. Why didn't you marry her?'

'Ah, now, honey,' he said. 'For heaven's sakes!'

'Why didn't you marry her?' she said. 'All you've done, ever since we got on this train, is talk about her. Here I've sat and sat, and just listened to you saying how wonderful Louise is. I suppose that's nice, getting me all off here alone with you, and then raving about Louise right in front of my face. Why didn't you ask her to marry you? I'm sure she would have jumped at the chance. There aren't so many people asking her to marry them. It's too bad you didn't marry her. I'm sure you'd have been much happier.'

'Listen, baby,' he said, 'while you're talking about things like that, why didn't you marry Joe Brooks? I suppose he could have given you all the twenty-two-dollar hats you wanted, I suppose!'

'Well, I'm not so sure I'm not sorry I didn't,' she said. 'There! Joe Brooks wouldn't have waited until he got me all off alone and then sneered at my taste in clothes. Joe Brooks wouldn't ever hurt my feelings. Joe Brooks has always been fond of me. There!'

'Yeah,' he said. 'He's fond of you. He was so fond of you he didn't even send a wedding present. That's how fond of you he was.'

'I happen to know for a fact,' she said, 'that he was away on business, and as soon as he comes back he's going to give me anything I want for the apartment.'

'Listen,' he said. 'I don't want anything he gives you in our apartment. Anything he gives you, I'll throw right out the window. That's what I think of your friend Joe Brooks. And how do you know where he is and what he's going to do, anyway? Has he been writing to you?'

'I suppose my friends can correspond with me,' she said. 'I didn't hear there was any law against that.'

'Well, I suppose they can't!' he said. 'And what do you think of that? I'm not going to have my wife getting a lot of letters from cheap travelling salesmen!'

'Joe Brooks is not a cheap travelling salesman!' she said. 'He is not! He gets a wonderful salary.'

'Oh yeah?' he said. 'Where did you hear that?'

'He told me so himself,' she said.

'Oh, he told you so himself,' he said. 'I see. He told you so himself.'

'You've got a lot of right to talk about Joe Brooks,' she said. 'You and your friend Louise. All you ever talk about is Louise.'

'Oh, for heaven's sakes!' he said. 'What do I care about Louise? I just thought she was a friend of yours, that's all. That's why I ever even noticed her.'

'Well, you certainly took an awful lot of notice of her today,' she said. 'On our wedding day! You said yourself when you were standing there in the church you just kept thinking of her. Right up at the altar. Oh, right in the presence of God! And all you thought about was Louise.'

'Listen, honey,' he said, 'I never should have said that. How does anybody know what kind of crazy things come into their heads when they're standing there waiting to get married? I was just telling you that because it was so kind of crazy. I thought it would make you laugh.'

'I know,' she said. 'I've been all sort of mixed up today, too. I told you that. Everything so strange and everything. And me all the time thinking about all those people all over the world, and now us here all alone, and everything. I know you get all mixed up. Only I did think, when you kept talking about how beautiful Louise looked, you did it with malice and forethought.'

'I never did anything with malice and forethought!' he said. 'I just told you that about Louise because I thought it would make you laugh.'

'Well, it didn't,' she said.

'No, I know it didn't,' he said. 'It certainly did not. Ah, baby, and we ought to be laughing, too. Hell, honey lamb, this is our honeymoon. What's the matter?'

'I don't know,' she said. 'We used to squabble a lot when we were going together and then engaged and everything, but I thought everything would be so different as soon as you were married. And now I feel so sort of strange and everything. I feel so sort of alone.'

'Well, you see, sweetheart,' he said, 'we're not really married yet. I mean. I mean – well, things will be different afterwards. Oh, hell. I mean, we haven't been married very long.'

'No,' she said.

'Well, we haven't got much longer to wait now,' he said. 'I mean – well, we'll be in New York in about twenty minutes. Then we can have dinner, and sort of see what we feel like doing. Or I mean. Is there anything special you want to do tonight?'

'What?' she said.

'What I mean to say,' he said, 'would you like to go to a show or something?'

'Why, whatever you like,' she said. 'I sort of didn't think people went to theatres and things on their – I mean, I've got a couple of letters I simply must write. Don't let me forget.'

'Oh,' he said. 'You're going to write letters tonight?'

'Well, you see,' she said. 'I've been perfectly terrible. What with all the excitement and everything. I never did thank poor old Mrs Sprague for her berry spoon, and I never did a thing about those bookends the McMasters sent. It's just too awful of me. I've got to write them this very night.'

'And when you've finished writing your letters,' he said, 'maybe I could get you a magazine or a bag of peanuts.'

'What?' she said.

'I mean,' he said, 'I wouldn't want you to be bored.'

'As if I could be bored with you!' she said. 'Silly! Aren't we married? Bored!'

'What I thought,' he said, 'I thought when we got in, we could go right up to the Biltmore and anyway leave our bags, and maybe have a little dinner in the room, kind of quiet, and then do whatever we wanted. I mean. I mean – well, let's go right up there from the station.'

'Oh, yes, let's,' she said. 'I'm so glad we're going to the Biltmore. I just love it. The twice I've stayed in New York we've always stayed there, Papa and Mamma and Ellie and I, and I was crazy about it. I always sleep so well there. I go right off to sleep the minute I put my head on the pillow.'

'Oh, you do?' he said.

'At least, I mean,' she said. ' 'Way up high it's so quiet.'

'We might go to some show or other tomorrow night instead of tonight,' he said. 'Don't you think that would be better?'

'Yes, I think it might,' she said.

He rose, balanced a moment, crossed over and sat down beside her.

'Do you really have to write those letters tonight?' he said.

'Well,' she said, 'I don't suppose they'd get there any quicker than if I wrote them tomorrow.'

There was a silence with things going on in it.

'And we won't ever fight any more, will we?' he said.

'Oh, no,' she said. 'Not ever! I don't know what made me do like that. It all got so sort of funny, sort of like a nightmare, the way I got thinking of all those people getting married all the time; and so many of them, everything spoils on account of fighting and everything. I got all mixed up thinking about them. Oh, I don't want to be like them. But we won't be, will we?'

'Sure we won't,' he said.

'We won't go all to pieces,' she said. 'We won't fight. It'll all be different, now we're married. It'll all be lovely. Reach me down my hat, will you, sweetheart? It's time I was putting it on. Thanks. Ah, I'm so sorry you don't like it.'

'I do so like it!' he said.

'You said you didn't,' she said. 'You said you thought it was perfectly terrible.'

'I never said any such thing,' he said. 'You're crazy.'

'All right, I may be crazy,' she said. 'Thank you very much. But that's what you said. Not that it matters – it's just a little thing. But it makes you feel pretty funny to think you've gone and married somebody that says you have perfectly terrible taste in hats. And then goes and says you're crazy, beside.'

'Now, listen here,' he said. 'Nobody said any such thing. Why, I love that hat. The more I look at it the better I like it. I think it's great.'

'That isn't what you said before,' she said.

'Honey,' he said. 'Stop it, will you? What do you want to start all this for? I love the damned hat. I mean, I love your hat. I love anything you wear. What more do you want me to say?'

'Well, I don't want you to say it like that,' she said.

'I said I think it's great,' he said. 'That's all I said.'

'Do you really?' she said. 'Do you honestly? Ah, I'm so glad. I'd hate you not to like my hat. It would be – I don't know, it would be sort of such a bad start.'

'Well, I'm crazy for it,' he said. 'Now we've got that settled, for heaven's sakes. Ah, baby. Baby lamb. We're not going to have any bad starts. Look at us – we're on our honeymoon. Pretty soon we'll be regular old married people. I mean. I mean, in a few minutes we'll be getting in to New York, and then we'll be going to the hotel, and then everything will be all right. I mean – well, look at us! Here we are married! Here we are!'

'Yes, here we are,' she said. 'Aren't we?'

The Reticence of Lady Anne

EGBERT came into the large dimly lit drawing-room with the air of a man who is not certain whether he is entering a dovecote or a bomb factory, and is prepared for either eventuality. The little domestic quarrel over the luncheon-table had not been fought to a definite finish, and the question was how far Lady Anne was in a mood to renew or forgo hostilities. Her pose in the arm-chair by the tea-table was rather elaborately rigid; in the gloom of a December afternoon Egbert's pince-nez did not materially help him to discern the expression of her face.

By way of breaking whatever ice might be floating on the surface he made a remark about a dim religious light. He or Lady Anne were accustomed to make that remark between 4.30 and 6.0 on winter and late autumn evenings; it was a part of their married life. There was no recognized rejoinder to it, and Lady Anne made none.

Don Tarquinio lay astretch on the Persian rug, basking in the firelight with superb indifference to the possible ill-humour of Lady Anne. His pedigree was as flawlessly Persian as the rug, and his ruff was coming into the glory of its second winter. The page-boy, who had Renaissance tendencies, had christened him Don Tarquinio. Left to themselves, Egbert and Lady Anne would unfailingly have called him Fluff, but they were not obstinate.

Egbert poured himself out some tea. As the silence gave no sign of breaking on Lady Anne's initiative, he braced himself for another Yermak effort.

'My remark at lunch had a purely academic application,' he announced; 'you seem to put an unnecessarily personal significance into it.'

Lady Anne maintained her defensive barrier of silence. The bullfinch lazily filled in the interval with an air from *Iphigénie en Tauride*. Egbert recognized it immediately, because it was the only air the bullfinch whistled, and he had come to them with the reputation for whistling it. Both Egbert and Lady Anne would have preferred something from *The Yeomen of the Guard*, which was their favourite opera. In matters artistic they had a similarity of taste. They leaned towards the honest and explicit in art, a picture, for instance, that told its own story, with generous assistance from its title. A riderless warhorse with harness in obvious disarray, staggering into a courtyard full of pale swooning women, and marginally noted 'Bad News', suggested to their minds a distinct interpretation of some military catastrophe. They could see what it was meant to convey, and explain it to friends of duller intelligence.

The silence continued. As a rule Lady Anne's displeasure became articulate and markedly voluble after four minutes of introductory muteness. Egbert seized the milk-jug and poured some of its contents into Don Tarquinio's saucer; as the saucer was already full to the brim an unsightly overflow was the result. Don Tarquinio looked on with a surprised interest that evanesced into elaborate unconsciousness when he was appealed to by Egbert to come and drink up some of the spilt matter. Don Tarquinio was prepared to play many rôles in life, but a vacuum carpet-cleaner was not one of them.

'Don't you think we're being rather foolish?' said Egbert cheerfully.

If Lady Anne thought so she didn't say so.

'I daresay the fault has been partly on my side,' continued Egbert, with evaporating cheerfulness. 'After all, I'm only human, you know. You seem to forget that I'm only human.'

He insisted on the point, as if there had been unfounded suggestions that he was built on Satyr lines, with goat continuations where the human left off.

The bullfinch recommenced its air from *Iphigénie en Tauride*.

Egbert began to feel depressed. Lady Anne was not drinking her tea. Perhaps she was feeling unwell. But when Lady Anne felt unwell she was not wont to be reticent on the subject. 'No one knows what I suffer from indigestion' was one of her favourite statements; but the lack of knowledge can only have been caused by defective listening; the amount of information available on the subject would have supplied material for a monograph.

Evidently Lady Anne was not feeling unwell.

Egbert began to think he was being unreasonably dealt with; naturally he began to make concessions.

'I daresay,' he observed, taking as central a position on the hearth-rug as Don Tarquinio could be persuaded to concede him, 'I may have been to blame. I am willing, if I can thereby restore things to a happier standpoint, to undertake to lead a better life.'

He wondered vaguely how it would be possible. Temptations came to him, in middle age, tentatively and without insistence, like a neglected butcher-boy who asks for a Christmas box in February for no more hopeful reason than that he didn't get one in December. He had no more idea of succumbing to them than he had of purchasing the fish-knives and fur boas that ladies are impelled to sacrifice through the medium of advertisement columns during twelve months of the year. Still, there was something impressive in this unasked-for renunciation of possibly latent enormities.

Lady Anne showed no sign of being impressed.

Egbert looked at her nervously through his glasses. To get the worst of an argument with her was no new experience. To get the worst of a monologue was a humiliating novelty.

'I shall go and dress for dinner,' he announced in a voice into which he intended some shade of sternness to creep.

At the door a final access of weakness impelled him to make a further appeal.

'Aren't we being very silly?'

'A fool,' was Don Tarquinio's mental comment as the door closed on Egbert's retreat. Then he lifted his velvet forepaws in the air and leapt lightly on to a bookshelf immediately under the bullfinch's cage. It was the first time he had seemed to notice the bird's existence, but he was carrying out a long-formed theory of action with the precision of mature deliberation. The bullfinch, who had fancied himself something of a despot, depressed himself of a sudden into a third of his normal displacement; then he fell to a helpless wing-beating and shrill cheeping. He had cost twenty-seven shillings without the cage, but Lady Anne made no sign of interfering. She had been dead for two hours.

DISCOMFITURE

Clothe the Naked

BIG LANNIE went out by the day to the houses of secure and leisured ladies, to wash their silks and their linens. She did her work perfectly; some of the ladies even told her so. She was a great, slow mass of a woman, coloured a sound brown-black save for her palms and the flat of her fingers that were like gutta-percha from steam and hot suds. She was slow because of her size, and because the big veins in her legs hurt her, and her back ached much of the time. She neither cursed her ills nor sought remedies for them. They had happened to her; there they were.

Many things had happened to her. She had had children, and the children had died. So had her husband, who was a kind man, cheerful with the little luck he found. None of their children had died at birth. They had lived to be four or seven or ten, so that they had had their ways and their traits and their means of causing love; and Big Lannie's heart was always wide for love. One child had been killed in a street accident and two others had died of illnesses that might have been no more than tedious, had there been fresh food and clear spaces and clean air behind them. Only Arlene, the youngest, lived to grow up.

Arlene was a tall girl, not so dark as her mother but with the same firm flatness of colour. She was so thin that her bones seemed to march in advance of her body. Her little pipes of legs and her broad feet with jutting heels were like things a child draws with crayons. She carried her head low, her shoulders scooped around her chest, and her stomach slanted forward. From the time that she was tiny, there were men after her.

Arlene was a bad girl always; that was one of the things that had happened to Big Lannie. There it was, and Big Lannie could only keep bringing her presents, surprises, so that the girl would love her mother and would want to stay at home. She brought little bottles of sharp perfume, and pale stockings of tinny silk, and rings set with bits of green and red glass; she tried to choose what Arlene would like. But each time Arlene came home she had bigger rings and softer stockings and stronger perfume than her mother could buy for her. Sometimes she would stay with her mother over a night, and sometimes more than a week; and then Big Lannie would come back from work one evening, and the girl would be gone, and no word of her. Big Lannie would go on bringing surprises, and setting them out along Arlene's bed to wait a return.

Big Lannie did not know it, when Arlene was going to have a baby. Arlene had not been home in nearly half a year; Big Lannie told the time in days. There was no news at all of the girl until the people at the hospital sent for Big Lannie to come to her daughter and grandson. She was there to hear Arlene say the baby must be named Raymond, and to see the girl die. For whom Raymond was called, or if anyone, Big Lannie never knew.

He was a long, light-coloured baby, with big milky eyes that looked right back at his grandmother. It was several days before the people at the hospital told her he was blind.

Big Lannie went to each of the ladies who employed her and explained that she could not work for some while; she must take care of her grandson. The ladies were sharply discommoded, after her steady years, but they dressed their outrage in shrugs and cool tones. Each arrived, separately, at the conclusion that she had been too good to Big Lannie, and had been imposed upon, therefore. 'Honestly, those niggers!' each said to her friends. 'They're all alike.'

Big Lannie sold most of the things she lived with, and took one room with a stove in it. There, as soon as the people at the hospital would let her, she brought Raymond and tended him. He was all her children to her.

She had always been a saving woman, with few needs and no cravings, and she had been long alone. Even after Arlene's burial, there was enough left for Raymond and Big Lannie to go on for a time. Big Lannie was slow to be afraid of what must come; fear did not visit her at all, at first, and then it slid in only when she waked, when the night hung motionless before another day.

Raymond was a good baby, a quiet, patient baby, lying in his wooden box and stretching out his delicate hands to the sounds that were light and colour to him. It seemed but a little while, so short to Big Lannie, before he was walking about the room, his hands held out, his feet quick and sure. Those of Big Lannie's friends who saw him for the first time had to be told that he could not see.

Then, and it seemed again such a little while, he could dress himself, and open the door for his granny, and unlace the shoes from her tired feet, and talk to her in his soft voice. She had occasional employment – now and then a neighbour would hear of a day's scrubbing she could do, or sometimes she might work in the stead of a friend who was sick – infrequent, and not to be planned on. She went to the ladies for whom she had worked, to ask if they might not want her back again; but there was little hope in her, after she had visited the first one. Well, now, really, said the ladies; well, really, now.

The neighbours across the hall watched over Raymond while Big Lannie looked for work. He was no trouble to them, nor to himself. He sat and crooned at his chosen task. He had been given a wooden spool around the top of which were driven little brads, and over these with a straightened hairpin he looped bright worsted, working faster than sight until a long tube of woven wool fell through the hole in the spool. The neighbours threaded big, blunt needles for him, and he coiled the woollen tubes and sewed them into mats. Big Lannie called them beautiful, and it made Raymond proud to have her tell him how readily she sold them. It was hard for her, when he was asleep at night, to unravel the mats and wash the worsted and stretch it so straight that even Raymond's shrewd fingers could not tell, when he worked with it next day, that it was not new.

Fear stormed in Big Lannie and took her days and nights. She might not go to any organization dispensing relief, for dread that Raymond would be taken from her and put in – she would not say the word to herself, and she and her neighbours lowered their voices when they said it to one another – an institution. The neighbours wove lingering tales of what happened inside certain neat, square buildings on the cindery skirts of the town, and, if they must go near them, hurried as if passing graveyards, and came home heroes. When they got you in one of those places, whispered the neighbours, they laid your spine open with whips, and then when you dropped, they kicked your head in. Had anyone come into Big Lannie's room to take Raymond away to an asylum for the blind, the neighbours would have fought for him with stones and rails and boiling water.

Raymond did not know about anything but good. When he grew big enough to go alone down the stairs and into the street, he was certain of delight each day. He held his head high, as he came out into the little yard in front of the flimsy wooden house, and slowly turned his face from side to side, as if the air were soft liquid in which he bathed it. Trucks and wagons did not visit the street, which ended in a dump for rusted bedsprings and broken boilers and staved-in kettles; children played over its cobbles, and men and women sat talking in open windows and called across to one another in gay, rich voices. There was always laughter for Raymond to hear, and he would laugh back, and hold out his hands to it.

At first, the children stopped their play when he came out, and gathered quietly about him, and watched him, fascinated. They had been told of his affliction, and they had a sort of sickened pity for him. Some of them spoke to him, in soft, careful tones. Raymond would laugh with pleasure, and stretch his hands, the curious smooth, flat hands of the blind, to their voices. They would draw sharply back, afraid that his strange hands might touch them. Then, somehow ashamed because they had shrunk from him and he could not see that they had done so, they said gentle good-byes to him, and backed away into the street again, watching him steadily.

When they were gone, Raymond would start on his walk to the end of the street. He guided himself by lightly touching the broken fences along the dirt sidewalk, and as he walked he crooned little songs with no words to them. Some of the men and women at the windows would call hello to him, and he would call back and wave and smile. When the children, forgetting him, laughed again at their games, he stopped and turned to the sound as if it were the sun.

In the evening, he would tell Big Lannie about his walk, slapping his knee and chuckling at the memory of the laughter he had heard. When the weather was too hard for him to go out in the street, he would sit at his worsted work, and talk all day of going out the next day.

The neighbours did what they could for Raymond and Big Lannie. They gave Raymond clothes their own children had not yet worn out, and they brought food, when they had enough to spare, and other things. Big Lannie would get through a week, and would pray to get through the next one; and so the months went. Then the days on which she could find work fell farther and farther apart, and she could not pray about the time to come because she did not dare to think of it.

It was Mrs Ewing who saved Raymond's and Big Lannie's lives, and let them continue together. Big Lannie said that then and ever after; daily she blessed Mrs Ewing, and nightly she would have prayed for her, had she not known, in some dimmed way, that any intercession for Mrs Delabarre Ewing must be impudence.

Mrs Ewing was a personage in the town. When she went to Richmond for a visit, or when she returned from viewing the azalea gardens in Charleston, the newspaper always printed the fact. She was a woman rigorously conscious of her noble obligation; she was prominent on the Community Chest committee, and it was she who planned and engineered the annual Bridge Drive to raise funds for planting salvia around the cannon in front of the

D.A.R. headquarters. These and many others were her public activities, and she was no less exacting of herself in her private life. She kept a model, though childless, house for her husband and herself, relegating the supervision of details to no domestic lieutenant, no matter how seemingly trustworthy.

Back before Raymond was born, Big Lannie had worked as laundress for Mrs Ewing. Since those days, the Ewing wash tubs had witnessed many changes, none for the better. Mrs Ewing took Big Lannie back into her employment. She apologized for this step to her friends by the always winning method of self-deprecation. She knew she was a fool, she said, after all that time, and after the way that Big Lannie had treated her. But still, she said – and she laughed a little at her own ways – anyone she felt kind of sorry for could always get around her, she said. She knew it was awful foolish, but that, she said, was the way she was. Mr Ewing, she said behind her husband's hearing, always called her just a regular little old easy mark.

Big Lannie had no words in which to thank Mrs Ewing, nor to tell her what two days' assured employment every week could mean. At least, it was fairly assured. Big Lannie, as Mrs Ewing pointed out to her, had got no younger, and she had always been slow. Mrs Ewing kept her in a state of stimulating insecurity by referring, with perfect truth, to the numbers of stronger, quicker women who were also in need of work.

Two days' work in the week meant money for rent and stovewood and almost enough food for Raymond and Big Lannie. She must depend, for anything further, on whatever odd jobs she could find, and she must not stop seeking them. Pressed on by fear and gratitude, she worked so well for Mrs Ewing that there was sometimes expressed satisfaction at the condition of the lady's household linen and her own and her husband's clothing. Big Lannie had a glimpse of Mr Ewing occasionally, leaving the house as she came, or entering it as she was leaving. He was a bit of a man, not much bigger than Raymond.

Raymond grew so fast that he seemed to be taller each morning.

Every day he had his walk in the street to look forward to and experience, and tell Big Lannie about at night. He had ceased to be a sight of the street; the children were so used to him that they did not even look at him, and the men and women at the windows no longer noticed him enough to hail him. He did not know. He would wave to any gay cry he heard, and go on his way, singing his little songs and turning toward the sound of laughter.

Then his lovely list of days ended as sharply as if ripped from some bright calendar. A winter came, so sudden and savage as to find no comparison in the town's memories, and Raymond had no clothes to wear out in the street. Big Lannie mended his outgrown garments as long as she could, but the stuff had so rotted with wear that it split in new places when she tried to sew together the ragged edges of rents.

The neighbours could give no longer; all they had they must keep for their own. A demented coloured man in a near-by town had killed the woman who employed him, and terror had spread like brush fire. There was a sort of panic of reprisal; coloured employees were dismissed from their positions, and there was no new work for them. But Mrs Ewing, admittedly soft-hearted certainly to a fault and possibly to a peril, kept her black laundress on. More than ever Big Lannie had reason to call her blessed.

All winter, Raymond stayed indoors. He sat at his spool and worsted, with Big Lannie's old sweater about his shoulders and, when his tattered knickerbockers would no longer hold together, a calico skirt of hers lapped around his waist. He lived, at his age, in the past; in the days when he had walked, proud and glad, in the street, with laughter in his ears. Always, when he talked of it, he must laugh back at that laughter.

Since he could remember, he had not been allowed to go out when Big Lannie thought the weather unfit. This he had accepted without question, and so he accepted his incarceration through the mean weeks of the winter. But then one day it was spring, so surely that he could tell it even in the smoky, stinking rooms of the house, and he cried out with joy because now he might walk in the street again. Big Lannie had to explain to him that his rags were too thin to shield him, and that there were no odd jobs for her, and so no clothes and shoes for him.

Raymond did not talk about the street any more, and his fingers were slow at his spool.

Big Lannie did something she had never done before; she begged of her employer. She asked Mrs Ewing to give her some of Mr Ewing's old clothes for Raymond. She looked at the floor and mumbled so that Mrs Ewing requested her to talk *up*. When Mrs Ewing understood, she was, she said, surprised. She had, she said, a great, great many demands on her charity, and she would have supposed that Big Lannie, of all people, might have known that she did everything she could, and, in fact, a good deal more. She spoke of inches and ells. She said that if she found she could spare anything, Big Lannie was kindly to remember it was to be just for this once.

When Big Lannie was leaving at the end of her day's work, Mrs Ewing brought her a package with her own hands. There, she said, was a suit and a pair of shoes; beautiful, grand things that people would think she was just a crazy to go giving away like that. She simply didn't know, she said, what Mr Ewing would say to her for being such a crazy. She explained that that was the way she was when anyone got around her, all the while Big Lannie was trying to thank her.

Big Lannie had never before seen Raymond behave as he did when she brought him home the package. He jumped and danced and clapped his hands, he tried to speak and squealed instead, he tore off the paper himself, and ran his fingers over the close-woven cloth and held it to his face and kissed it. He put on the shoes and clattered about in them, digging with his toes and heels to keep them on; he made Big Lannie pin the trousers around his waist and roll them up over his shins. He babbled of the morrow when he would walk in the street, and could not say his words for laughing.

Big Lannie must work for Mrs Ewing the next day, and she had thought to bid Raymond wait until she could stay at home and dress him herself in his new garments. But she heard him laugh again; she could not tell him he must wait. He might go out at noon next day, she said, when the sun was so warm that he would not take cold at his first outing; one of the neighbours across the hall would help him with the clothes. Raymond chuckled and sang his little songs until he went to sleep.

After Big Lannie left in the morning, the neighbour came in to Raymond, bringing a pan of cold pork and corn bread for his lunch. She had a call for a half-day's work, and she could not stay to see him start out for his walk. She helped him put on the trousers and pinned and rolled them for him, and she laced the shoes as snug as they would go on his feet. Then she told him not to go out till the noon whistles blew, and kissed him, and left.

Raymond was too happy to be impatient. He sat and thought of the street and smiled and sang. Not until he heard the whistles did he go to the drawer where Big Lannie had laid the coat, and take it out and put it on. He felt it soft on his bare back, he twisted his shoulders to let it fall warm and loose from them. As he folded the sleeves back over his thin arms, his heart beat so that the cloth above it fluttered.

The stairs were difficult for him to manage, in the big shoes, but the very slowness of the descent was delicious to him. His anticipation was like honey in his mouth.

Then he came out into the yard, and turned his face in the gentle air. It was all good again; it was all given back again. As quickly as he could, he gained the walk and set forth, guiding himself by the fence. He could not wait; he called out, so that he would hear gay calls in return, he laughed so that laughter would answer him.

He heard it. He was so glad that he took his hand from the fence and turned and stretched out his arms and held up his smiling face to welcome it. He stood there, and his smile died on his face, and his welcoming arms stiffened and shook.

It was not the laughter he had known; it was not the laughter he had lived on. It was like great flails beating him flat, great prongs tearing his flesh from his bones. It was coming at him, to kill him. It drew slyly back, and then it smashed against him. It swirled around and over him, and he could not breathe. He screamed and tried to run out through it, and fell, and it licked over him, howling higher. His clothes unrolled, and his shoes flapped on his feet. Each time he could rise, he fell again. It was as if the street were perpendicular before him, and the laughter leaping at his back. He could not find the fence, he did not know which way he was turned. He lay screaming, in blood and dust and darkness.

When Big Lannie came home, she found him on the floor in a corner of the room, moaning and whimpering. He still wore his new clothes, cut and torn and dusty, and there was dried blood on his mouth and his palms. Her heart had leapt in alarm when he had not opened the door at her footstep, and she cried out so frantically to ask what had happened that she frightened him into wild weeping. She could not understand what he said; it was something about the street, and laughing at him, and make them go away, and don't let him go in the street no more, never in the street no more. She did not try to make him explain. She took him in her arms and rocked him, and told him, over and over, never mind, don't care, everything's all right. Neither he nor she believed her words.

But her voice was soft and her arms warm. Raymond's sobs softened, and trembled away. She held him, rocking silently and rhythmically, a long time. Then gently she set him on his feet, and took from his shoulders Mr Ewing's old full-dress coat.

The Mouse

THEODORIC VOLER had been brought up, from infancy to the confines of middle age, by a fond mother whose chief solicitude had been to keep him screened from what she called the coarser realities of life. When she died she left Theodoric alone in a world that was as real as ever, and a good deal coarser than he considered it had any need to be. To a man of his temperament and up-bringing even a simple railway journey was crammed with petty annoyances and minor discords, and as he settled himself down in a second-class compartment one September morning he was conscious of ruffled feelings and general mental discomposure. He had been staying at a country vicarage, the inmates of which had been certainly neither brutal nor bacchanalian, but their super-vision of the domestic establishment had been of that lax order which invites disaster. The pony carriage that was to take him to the station had never been properly ordered, and when the moment for his departure drew near the handy-man who should have produced the required article was nowhere to be found. In this emergency Theodoric, to his mute but very intense disgust, found himself obliged to collaborate with the vicar's daughter in the task of harnessing the pony, which necessitated groping about in an ill-lighted outhouse called a stable, and smelling very like one – except in patches where it smelt of mice. Without being actually afraid of mice, Theodoric classed them among the coarser incidents of life, and considered that Providence, with a little exercise of moral courage, might long ago have recognized that they were not indispensable, and have withdrawn them from circulation. As the train glided out of the station Theodoric's nervous imagination accused himself of exhaling a weak odour of stableyard, and possibly of displaying a mouldy straw or two on his usually well-brushed garments. Fortunately the only other occupant of the compartment, a lady of about the same age as himself, seemed inclined for slumber rather than scrutiny; the train was not due to stop till the terminus was reached, in about an hour's time, and the carriage was of the old-fashioned sort, that held no communication with a corridor, therefore no further travelling companions were likely to intrude on Theodoric's semi-privacy. And yet the train had scarcely attained its normal speed before he became reluctantly but vividly aware that he was not alone with the slumbering lady; he was not even alone in his own clothes. A warm, creeping movement over his flesh betrayed the unwelcome and highly resented presence, unseen but poignant, of a strayed mouse, that had evidently dashed into its present retreat during the episode of the pony harnessing. Furtive stamps and shakes and wildly directed pinches failed to dislodge the intruder, whose motto, indeed, seemed to be Excelsior; and the lawful occupant of the clothes lay back against the cushions and endeavoured rapidly to evolve some means for putting an end to the dual ownership. It was unthinkable that he should continue for the space of a whole hour in the horrible position of a Rowton House for vagrant mice (already his imagination had at least doubled the numbers of the alien invasion). On the other hand, nothing less drastic than partial disrobing would ease him of his tormentor, and to undress in the presence of a lady, even for so laudable a purpose, was an idea that made his eartips tingle in a blush of abject shame. He had never been able to bring himself even to the mild exposure of open-work socks in the presence of the fair sex. And yet – the lady in this case was to all appearances soundly and securely asleep; the mouse, on the other hand, seemed to be trying to crowd a Wanderjahr into a few strenuous minutes. If there is any truth in the theory of transmigration, this particular mouse must certainly have been in a former state a member of the Alpine Club. Sometimes in its eagerness it lost its footing and slipped for half an inch or so; and then, in fright, or more probably temper, it bit. Theodoric was goaded into the most audacious undertaking of his life. Crimsoning to the hue of a beetroot and keeping an agonized watch on his slumbering fellow-traveller, he swiftly and noiselessly secured the ends of his railway rug to the racks on either side of the carriage, so that a substantial curtain hung athwart the compartment. In the narrow dressing-room that he had thus improvised he proceeded with violent haste to extricate himself partially and the mouse entirely from the surrounding casings of tweed and half-wool. As the unravelled mouse gave a wild leap to the floor, the rug, slipping its fastening at either end, also came down with a heart-curdling flop, and almost simultaneously the awakened sleeper opened her eyes. With a movement almost quicker than the mouse's, Theodoric pounced on the rug, and hauled its ample folds chin-high over his dismantled person as he collapsed into the further corner of the carriage. The blood raced and beat in the veins of his neck and forehead, while he waited dumbly for the communication-cord to be pulled. The lady, however, contented herself with a silent stare at her strangely muffled companion. How much had she seen, Theodoric queried to himself, and in any case what on earth must she think of his present posture?

'I think I have caught a chill,' he ventured desperately.

'Really, I'm sorry,' she replied. 'I was just going to ask you if you would open this window.'

'I fancy it's malaria,' he added, his teeth chattering slightly, as much from fright as from a desire to support his theory.

'I've got some brandy in my hold-all, if you'll kindly reach it down for me,' said his companion.

'Not for worlds – I mean, I never take anything for it,' he assured her earnestly.

'I suppose you caught it in the Tropics?'

Theodoric, whose acquaintance with the Tropics was limited to an annual present of a chest of tea from an uncle in Ceylon, felt that even the malaria was slipping from him. Would it be possible, he wondered, to disclose the real state of affairs to her in small instalments?

'Are you afraid of mice?' he ventured, growing, if possible, more scarlet in the face.

'Not unless they come in quantities, like those that ate up Bishop Hatto. Why do you ask?'

'I had one crawling inside my clothes just now,' said Theodoric in a voice that hardly seemed his own. 'It was a most awkward situation.'

'It must have been, if you wear your clothes at all tight,' she observed; 'but mice have strange ideas of comfort.'

'I had to get rid of it while you were asleep,' he continued; then, with a gulp, he added, 'it was getting rid of it that brought me to – to this.'

'Surely leaving off one small mouse wouldn't bring on a chill,' she exclaimed, with a levity that Theodoric accounted abominable.

Evidently she had detected something of his predicament, and was enjoying his confusion. All the blood in his body seemed to have mobilized in one concentrated blush, and an agony of abasement, worse than a myriad mice, crept up and down over his soul. And then, as reflection began to assert itself, sheer terror took the place of humiliation. With every minute that passed the train was rushing nearer to the crowded and bustling terminus where dozens of prying eyes would be exchanged for the one paralysing pair that watched him from the further corner of the carriage. There was one slender despairing chance, which the next few minutes must decide. His fellow-traveller might relapse into a blessed slumber. But as the minutes throbbed by, that chance ebbed away. The furtive glance which Theodoric stole at her from time to time disclosed only an unwinking wakefulness.

'I think we must be getting near now,' she presently observed.

Theodoric had already noted with growing terror the recurring stacks of small, ugly dwellings that heralded the journey's end. The words acted as a signal. Like a hunted beast breaking cover and dashing madly towards some other haven of momentary safety he threw aside his rug, and struggled frantically into his dishevelled garments. He was conscious of dull suburban stations racing past the window, of a choking, hammering sensation in his throat and heart, and of an icy silence in that corner towards which he dared not look. Then as he sank back in his seat, clothed and almost delirious, the train slowed down to a final crawl, and the woman spoke.

'Would you be so kind,' she asked, 'as to get me a porter to put me into a cab? It's a shame to trouble you when you're feeling unwell, but being blind makes one so helpless at a railway station.'

Dusk

NORMAN GORTSBY sat on a bench in the Park, with his back to a strip of bush-planted sward, fenced by the park railings, and the Row fronting him across a wide stretch of carriage drive. Hyde Park Corner, with its rattle and hoot of traffic, lay immediately to his right. It was some thirty minutes past six on an early March evening, and dusk had fallen heavily over the scene, dusk mitigated by some faint moonlight and many street lamps. There was a wide emptiness over road and sidewalk, and yet there were many unconsidered figures moving silently through the half-light or dotted unobtrusively on bench and chair, scarcely to be distinguished from the shadowed gloom in which they sat.

The scene pleased Gortsby and harmonized with his present mood. Dusk, to his mind, was the hour of the defeated. Men and women, who had fought and lost, who hid their fallen fortunes and dead hopes as far as possible from the scrutiny of the curious, came forth in this hour of gloaming, when their shabby clothes and bowed shoulders and unhappy eyes might pass unnoticed, or, at any rate, unrecognized.

> A king that is conquered must see strange looks,
> So bitter a thing is the heart of man.

The wanderers in the dusk did not choose to have strange looks fasten on them, therefore they came out in this bat-fashion, taking their pleasure sadly in a pleasure-ground that had emptied of its rightful occupants. Beyond the sheltering screen of bushes and palings came a realm of brilliant lights and noisy, rushing traffic. A blazing, many-tiered stretch of windows shone through the dusk and almost dispersed it, marking the haunts of those other people, who held their own in life's struggle, or at any rate had not had to admit failure. So Gortsby's imagination pictured things as he sat on his bench in the almost deserted walk. He was in the mood to count himself among the defeated. Money troubles did not press on him; had he so wished he could have strolled into the thoroughfares of light and noise, and taken his place among the jostling ranks of those who enjoyed prosperity or struggled for it. He had failed in a more subtle ambition, and for the moment he was heart sore and disillusionized, and not disinclined to take a certain cynical pleasure in observing and labelling his fellow wanderers as they went their ways in the dark stretches between the lamp-lights.

On the bench by his side sat an elderly gentleman with a drooping air of defiance that was probably the remaining vestige of self-respect in an individual who had ceased to defy successfully anybody or anything. His clothes could scarcely be called shabby, at least they passed muster in the half-light, but one's imagination could not have pictured the wearer embarking on the purchase of a half-crown box of chocolates or laying out ninepence on a carnation buttonhole. He belonged unmistakably to that forlorn orchestra to whose piping no one dances; he was one of the world's lamenters who induces no responsive weeping. As he rose to go Gortsby imagined him returning to a home circle where he was snubbed and of no account, or to some bleak lodging where his ability to pay a weekly bill was the beginning and end of the interest he inspired. His retreating figure vanished slowly into the shadows, and his place on the bench was taken almost immediately by a young man, fairly well dressed but scarcely more cheerful of mien than his predecessor. As if to emphasize the fact that the world went badly with him the newcomer unburdened himself of an angry and very audible expletive as he flung himself into the seat.

'You don't seem in a very good temper,' said Gortsby, judging that he was expected to take due notice of the demonstration.

The young man turned to him with a look of disarming frankness which put him instantly on his guard.

'You wouldn't be in a good temper if you were in the fix I'm in,' he said; 'I've done the silliest thing I've ever done in my life.'

'Yes?' said Gortsby dispassionately.

'Came up this afternoon, meaning to stay at the Patagonian Hotel in Berkshire Square,' continued the young man; 'when I got there I found it had been pulled down some weeks ago and a cinema theatre run up on the site. The taxi driver recommended me to another hotel some way off and I went there. I just sent a letter to my people, giving them the address, and then I went out to buy some soap – I'd forgotten to pack any and I hate using hotel soap. Then I strolled about a bit, had a drink at a bar and looked at the shops, and when I came to turn my steps back to the hotel I suddenly realized that I didn't remember its name or even what street it was in. There's a nice predicament for a fellow who hasn't any friends or connections in London! Of course I can wire to my people for the address, but they won't have got my letter till tomorrow; meantime I'm without any money, came out with about a shilling on me, which went in buying the soap and getting the drink, and here I am, wandering about with twopence in my pocket and nowhere to go for the night.'

There was an eloquent pause after the story had been told. 'I suppose you think I've spun you rather an impossible yarn,' said the young man presently, with a suggestion of resentment in his voice.

'Not at all impossible,' said Gortsby judicially; 'I remember doing exactly the same thing once in a foreign capital, and on that occasion there were two of us, which made it more remarkable. Luckily we remembered that the hotel was on a sort of canal, and when we struck the canal we were able to find our way back to the hotel.'

The youth brightened at the reminiscence. 'In a foreign city, I wouldn't mind so much,' he said; 'one could go to one's Consul and get the requisite help from him. Here in one's own land one is far more derelict if one gets into a fix. Unless I can find some decent chap to swallow my story and lend me some money I seem likely to spend the night on the Embankment. I'm glad, anyhow, that you don't think the story outrageously improbable.'

He threw a good deal of warmth into the last remark, as though perhaps to indicate his hope that Gortsby did not fall far short of the requisite decency.

'Of course,' said Gortsby slowly, 'the weak point of your story is that you can't produce the soap.'

The young man sat forward hurriedly, felt rapidly in the pockets of his overcoat, and then jumped to his feet.

'I must have lost it,' he muttered angrily.

'To lose an hotel and a cake of soap on one afternoon suggests wilful carelessness,' said Gortsby, but the young man scarcely waited to hear the end of the remark. He flitted away down the path, his head held high, with an air of somewhat jaded jauntiness.

'It was a pity,' mused Gortsby; 'the going out to get one's own soap was the one convincing touch in the whole story, and yet it was just that little detail that brought him to grief. If he had had the brilliant forethought to provide himself with a cake of soap, wrapped and sealed with all the solicitude of the chemist's counter, he would have been a genius in his particular line. In his particular line genius certainly consists of an infinite capacity for taking precautions.'

With that reflection Gortsby rose to go; as he did so an exclamation of concern escaped him. Lying on the ground by the side of the bench was a small oval packet, wrapped and sealed with the solicitude of a chemist's counter. It could be nothing else but a cake of soap, and it had evidently fallen out of the youth's overcoat pocket when he flung himself down on the seat. In another moment Gortsby was scudding along the dusk-shrouded path in anxious quest for a youthful figure in a light overcoat. He had nearly given up the search when he caught sight of the object of his pursuit standing irresolutely on the border of the carriage drive, evidently uncertain whether to strike across the Park or make for the bustling pavements of Knightsbridge. He turned round sharply with an air of defensive hostility when he found Gortsby hailing him.

'The important witness to the genuineness of your story has turned up,' said Gortsby, holding out the cake of soap; 'it must have slid out of your overcoat pocket when you sat down on the seat. I saw it on the ground after you left. You must excuse my disbelief, but appearances were really rather against you, and now, as I appealed to the testimony of the soap I think I ought to abide by its verdict. If the loan of a sovereign is any good to you – "

The young man hastily removed all doubt on the subject by pocketing the coin.

'Here is my card with my address,' continued Gortsby; 'any day this week will do for returning the money, and here is the soap – don't lose it again; it's been a good friend to you.'

'Lucky thing your finding it,' said the youth, and then, with a catch in his voice, he blurted out a word or two of thanks and fled headlong in the direction of Knightsbridge.

'Poor boy, he as nearly as possible broke down,' said Gortsby to himself. 'I don't wonder either; the relief from his quandary must have been acute. It's a lesson to me not to be too clever in judging by circumstances.'

As Gortsby retraced his steps past the seat where the little drama had taken place he saw an elderly gentleman poking and peering beneath it and on all sides of it, and recognized his earlier fellow occupant.

'Have you lost anything, sir?' he asked.

'Yes, sir, a cake of soap.'

MAKE-BELIEVE

The Standard of Living

ANNABEL and Midge came out of the tea room with the arrogant slow gait of the leisured, for their Saturday afternoon stretched ahead of them. They had lunched, as was their wont, on sugar, starches, oils, and butter-fats. Usually they ate sandwiches of spongy new white bread greased with butter and mayonnaise; they ate thick wedges of cake lying wet beneath ice cream and whipped cream and melted chocolate gritty with nuts. As alternates, they ate patties, sweating beads of inferior oil, containing bits of bland meat bogged in pale, stiffening sauce; they ate pastries, limber under rigid icing, filled with an indeterminate yellow sweet stuff, not still solid, not yet liquid, like salve that has been left in the sun. They chose no other sort of food, nor did they consider it. And their skin was like the petals of wood anemones, and their bellies were as flat and their flanks as lean as those of young Indian braves.

Annabel and Midge had been best friends almost from the day that Midge had found a job as stenographer with the firm that employed Annabel. By now, Annabel, two years longer in the stenographic department, had worked up to the wages of eighteen dollars and fifty cents a week; Midge was still at sixteen dollars. Each girl lived at home with her family and paid half her salary to its support.

The girls sat side by side at their desks, they lunched together every noon, together they set out for home at the end of the day's work. Many of their evenings and most of their Sundays were passed in each other's company. Often they were joined by two young men, but there was no steadiness to any such quartet; the two young men would give place, unlamented, to two other young men, and lament would have been inappropriate, really, since the newcomers were scarcely distinguishable from their predecessors. Invariably the girls spent the fine idle hours of their hot-weather Saturday afternoons together. Constant use had not worn ragged the fabric of their friendship.

They looked alike, though the resemblance did not lie in their features. It was in the shape of their bodies, their movements, their style, and their adornments. Annabel and Midge did, and completely, all that young office workers are besought not to do. They painted their lips and their nails, they darkened their lashes and lightened their hair, and scent seemed to shimmer from them. They wore thin, bright dresses, tight over their breasts and high on their legs, and tilted slippers, fancifully strapped. They looked conspicuous and cheap and charming.

Now, as they walked across to Fifth Avenue with their skirts swirled by the hot wind, they received audible admiration. Young men grouped lethargically about news-stands awarded them murmurs, exclamations, even – the ultimate tribute – whistles. Annabel and Midge passed without the condescension of hurrying their pace; they held their heads higher and set their feet with exquisite precision, as if they stepped over the necks of peasants.

Always the girls went to walk on Fifth Avenue on their free afternoons, for it was the ideal ground for their favourite game. The game could be played anywhere, and, indeed, was, but the great shop windows stimulated the two players to their best form.

Annabel had invented the game; or rather she had evolved it from an old one. Basically, it was no more than the ancient sport of what-would-you-do-if-you-had-a-million-dollars? But Annabel had drawn a new set of rules for it, had narrowed it, pointed it, made it stricter. Like all games, it was the more absorbing for being more difficult.

Annabel's version went like this: You must suppose that somebody dies and leaves you a million dollars, cool. But there is a condition to the bequest. It is stated in the will that you must spend every nickel of the money on yourself.

There lay the hazard of the game. If, when playing it, you forgot, and listed among your expenditures the rental of a new apartment for your family, for example, you lost your turn to the other player. It was astonishing how many – and some of them among the experts, too – would forfeit all their innings by such slips.

It was essential, of course, that it be played in passionate seriousness. Each purchase must be carefully considered and, if necessary, supported by argument. There was no zest to playing wildly. Once Annabel had introduced the game to Sylvia, another girl who worked in the office. She explained the rules to Sylvia and then offered her the gambit 'What would be the first thing you'd do?' Sylvia had not shown the decency of even a second of hesitation. 'Well,' she said, 'the first thing I'd do, I'd go out and hire somebody to shoot Mrs Gary Cooper, and then . . .' So it is to be seen that she was no fun.

But Annabel and Midge were surely born to be comrades, for Midge played the game like a master from the moment she learned it. It was she who added the touches that made the whole thing cozier. According to Midge's innovations, the eccentric who died and left you the money was not anybody you loved, or, for the matter of that, anybody you even knew. It was somebody who had seen you somewhere and had thought, 'That girl ought to have lots of nice things. I'm going to leave her a million dollars when I die.' And the death was to be neither untimely nor painful. Your benefactor, full of years and comfortably ready to depart, was to slip softly away during sleep and go right to heaven. These embroideries permitted Annabel and Midge to play their game in the luxury of peaceful consciences.

Midge played with a seriousness that was not only proper but extreme. The single strain on the girls' friendship had followed an announcement once made by Annabel that the first thing she would buy with her million dollars would be a silver-fox coat. It was as if she had struck Midge across the mouth. When Midge recovered her breath, she cried that she couldn't imagine how

Annabel could do such a thing – silver-fox coats were common! Annabel defended her taste with the retort that they were not common, either. Midge then said that they were so. She added that everybody had a silver-fox coat. She went on, with perhaps a slight toss of head, to declare that she herself wouldn't be caught dead in silver fox.

For the next few days, though the girls saw each other as constantly, their conversation was careful and infrequent, and they did not once play their game. Then one morning, as soon as Annabel entered the office, she came to Midge and said that she had changed her mind. She would not buy a silver-fox coat with any part of her million dollars. Immediately on receiving the legacy, she would select a coat of mink.

Midge smiled and her eyes shone. 'I think,' she said, 'you're doing absolutely the right thing.'

Now, as they walked along Fifth Avenue, they played the game anew. It was one of those days with which September is repeatedly cursed; hot and glaring, with slivers of dust in the wind. People drooped and shambled, but the girls carried themselves tall and walked a straight line, as befitted young heiresses on their afternoon promenade. There was no longer need for them to start the game at its formal opening. Annabel went direct to the heart of it.

'All right,' she said. 'So you've got this million dollars. So what would be the first thing you'd do?'

'Well, the first thing I'd do,' Midge said, 'I'd get a mink coat.' But she said it mechanically, as if she were giving the memorized answer to an expected question.

'Yes,' Annabel said, 'I think you ought to. The terribly dark kind of mink.' But she, too, spoke as if by rote. It was too hot; fur, no matter how dark and sleek and supple, was horrid to the thoughts.

They stepped along in silence for a while. Then Midge's eye was caught by a shop window. Cool, lovely gleamings were there set off by chaste and elegant darkness.

'No,' Midge said, 'I take it back. I wouldn't get a mink coat the first thing. Know what I'd do? I'd get a string of pearls. Real pearls.'

Annabel's eyes turned to follow Midge's.

'Yes,' she said, slowly. 'I think that's a kind of a good idea. And it would make sense, too. Because you can wear pearls with anything.'

Together they went over to the shop window and stood pressed against it. It contained but one object – a double row of great, even pearls clasped by a deep emerald around a little pink velvet throat.

'What do you suppose they cost?' Annabel said.

'Gee, I don't know,' Midge said. 'Plenty, I guess.'

'Like a thousand dollars?' Annabel said.

'Oh, I guess like more,' Midge said. 'On account of the emerald.'

'Well, like ten thousand dollars?' Annabel said.

'Gee, I wouldn't even know,' Midge said.

The devil nudged Annabel in the ribs. 'Dare you to go in and price them,' she said.

'Like fun!' Midge said.

'Dare you,' Annabel said.

'Why, a store like this wouldn't even be open this afternoon,' Midge said.

'Yes, it is so, too,' Annabel said. 'People just came out. And there's a doorman on. Dare you.'

'Well,' Midge said. 'But you've got to come too.'

They tendered thanks, icily, to the doorman for ushering them into the shop. It was cool and quiet, a broad, gracious room with panelled walls and soft carpet. But the girls wore expressions of bitter disdain, as if they stood in a sty.

A slim, immaculate clerk came to them and bowed. His neat face showed no astonishment at their appearance.

'Good afternoon,' he said. He implied that he would never forget it if they would grant him the favour of accepting his soft-spoken greeting.

'Good afternoon,' Annabel and Midge said together, and in like freezing accents.

'Is there something – ?' the clerk said.

'Oh, we're just looking,' Annabel said. It was as if she flung the words down from a dais.

The clerk bowed.

'My friend and myself merely happened to be passing,' Midge said, and stopped, seeming to listen to the phrase. 'My friend here and myself,' she went on, 'merely happened to be wondering how much are those pearls you've got in your window.'

'Ah, yes,' the clerk said. 'The double rope. That is two hundred and fifty thousand dollars, Madam.'

'I see,' Midge said.

The clerk bowed. 'An exceptionally beautiful necklace,' he said. 'Would you care to look at it?'

'No thank you,' Annabel said.

'My friend and myself merely happened to be passing,' Midge said.

They turned to go; to go, from their manner, where the tumbrel awaited them. The clerk sprang ahead and opened the door. He bowed as they swept by him.

The girls went on along the Avenue and disdain was still on their faces.

'Honestly!' Annabel said. 'Can you imagine a thing like that?'

'Two hundred and fifty thousand dollars!' Midge said. 'That's a quarter of a million dollars right there!'

'He's got his nerve!' Annabel said.

They walked on. Slowly the disdain went, slowly and completely as if drained from them, and with it went the regal carriage and tread. Their shoulders dropped and they dragged their feet; they bumped against each other, without notice or apology, and caromed away again. They were silent and their eyes were cloudy.

Suddenly Midge straightened her back, flung her head high, and spoke, clear and strong.

'Listen, Annabel,' she said. 'Look. Suppose there was this

terribly rich person, see? You don't know this person, but this person has seen you somewhere and wants to do something for you. Well, it's a terribly old person, see? And so this person dies, just like going to sleep, and leaves you ten million dollars. Now, what would be the first thing you'd do?'

Morlvera

THE Olympic Toy Emporium occupied a conspicuous frontage in an important West End street. It was happily named Toy Emporium, because one would never have dreamed of according it the familiar and yet pulse-quickening name of toyshop. There was an air of cold splendour and elaborate failure about the wares that were set out in its ample windows; they were the sort of toys that a tired shop-assistant displays and explains at Christmas-time to exclamatory parents and bored, silent children. The animal toys looked more like natural history models than the comfortable, sympathetic companions that one would wish, at a certain age, to take to bed with one, and to smuggle into the bathroom. The mechanical toys incessantly did things that no one could want a toy to do more than half a dozen times in its lifetime; it was a merciful reflection that in any right-minded nursery the lifetime would certainly be short.

Prominent among the elegantly dressed dolls that filled an entire section of the window frontage was a large hobble-skirted lady in a confection of peach-coloured velvet, elaborately set off with leopard-skin accessories, if one may use such a conveniently comprehensive word in describing an intricate feminine toilette. She lacked nothing that is to be found in a carefully detailed fashion-plate – in fact, she might be said to have something more than the average fashion-plate female possesses; in place of a vacant, expressionless stare she had character in her face. It must be admitted that it was bad character, cold, hostile, inquisitorial, with a sinister lowering of one eyebrow and a merciless hardness about the corners of the mouth. One might have imagined histories about her by the hour, histories in which unworthy ambition, the desire for money, and an entire absence of all decent feeling would play a conspicuous part.

As a matter of fact, she was not without her judges and biographers, even in this shop-window stage of her career. Emmeline, aged ten, and Bert, aged seven, had halted on the way from their obscure back street to the minnow-stocked water of St James's Park, and were critically examining the hobble-skirted doll, and dissecting her character in no very tolerant spirit. There is probably a latent enmity between the necessarily under-clad and the unnecessarily over-dressed, but a little kindness and good-fellowship on the part of the latter will often change the sentiment to admiring devotion; if the lady in peach-coloured velvet and leopard-skin had worn a pleasant expression in addition to her other elaborate furnishings, Emmeline at least might have respected and even loved her. As it was, she gave her a horrible reputation, based chiefly on a second-hand knowledge of gilded depravity derived from the conversation of those who were skilled in the art of novelette reading; Bert filled in a few damaging details from his own limited imagination.

'She's a bad lot, that one is,' declared Emmeline, after a long unfriendly stare; ' 'er 'usbind 'ates 'er.'

' 'E knocks 'er abart,' said Bert with enthusiasm.

'No, 'e don't, cos 'e's dead; she poisoned 'im slow and gradual, so that nobody didn't know. Now she wants to marry a lord, with 'eaps and 'eaps of money. 'E's got a wife already, but she's going to poison 'er, too.'

'She's a bad lot,' said Bert with growing hostility.

' 'Er mother 'ates her, and she's afraid of 'er, too, cos she's got a serkestic tongue; always talking serkesms, she is. She's greedy, too; if there's fish going, she eats 'er own share and 'er little girl's as well, though the little girl is dellikit.'

'She 'ad a little boy once,' said Bert, 'but she pushed 'im into the water when nobody wasn't looking.'

'No, she didn't,' said Emmeline, 'she sent 'im away to be kep'' by poor people, so 'er husbind wouldn't know where 'e was. They ill-treat 'im somethink cruel.'

'Wot's 'er nime?' asked Bert, thinking that it was time that so interesting a personality should be labelled.

' 'Er nime?' asked Emmeline, thinking hard, ' 'er nime's Morlvera.' It was as near as she could get to the name of an adventuress who figured prominently in a cinema drama. There was silence for a moment while the possibilities of the name were turned over in the children's minds.

'Those clothes she's got on ain't paid for, and never won't be,' said Emmeline; 'she thinks she'll get the rich lord to pay for 'em, but 'e won't. 'E's given 'er jools, 'underds of pounds' worth.'

' 'E won't pay for the clothes,' said Bert with conviction. Evidently there was some limit to the weak good nature of wealthy lords.

At that moment a motor carriage with liveried servants drew up at the emporium entrance; a large lady, with a penetrating and rather hurried manner of talking, stepped out, followed slowly and sulkily by a small boy, who had a very black scowl on his face and a very white sailor suit over the rest of him. The lady was continuing an argument which had probably commenced in Portman Square.

'Now, Victor, you are to come in and buy a nice doll for your cousin Bertha. She gave you a beautiful box of soldiers on your birthday, and you must give her a present on hers.'

'Bertha is a fat little fool,' said Victor, in a voice that was as loud as his mother's and had more assurance in it.

'Victor, you are not to say such things. Bertha is not a fool, and she is not in the least fat. You are to come in and choose a doll for her.'

The couple passed into the shop, out of view and hearing of the two back-street children.

'My, he is in a wicked temper,' explained Emmeline, but both she and Bert were inclined to side with him against the absent

Bertha, who was doubtless as fat and foolish as he had described her to be.

'I want to see some dolls,' said the mother of Victor to the nearest assistant; 'it's for a little girl of eleven.'

'A fat little girl of eleven,' added Victor by way of supplementary information.

'Victor, if you say such rude things about your cousin, you shall go to bed the moment we get home, without having any tea.'

'This is one of the newest things we have in dolls,' said the assistant, removing a hobble-skirted figure in peach-coloured velvet from the window; 'leopard-skin toque and stole, the latest fashion. You won't get anything newer than that anywhere. It's an exclusive design.'

'Look!' whispered Emmeline outside; 'they've bin and took Morlvera.'

There was a mingling of excitement and a certain sense of bereavement in her mind; she would have liked to gaze at that embodiment of overdressed depravity for just a little longer.

'I 'spect she's going away in a kerridge to marry the rich lord,' hazarded Bert.

'She's up to no good,' said Emmeline vaguely.

Inside the shop the purchase of the doll had been decided on.

'It's a beautiful doll, and Bertha will be delighted with it,' asserted the mother of Victor loudly.

'Oh, very well,' said Victor sulkily; 'you needn't have it stuck in a box and wait an hour while it's being done up into a parcel. I'll take it as it is, and we can go round to Manchester Square and give it to Bertha, and get the thing done with. That will save me the trouble of writing, "For dear Bertha, with Victor's love," on a bit of paper.'

'Very well,' said his mother, 'we can go to Manchester Square on our way home. You must wish her many happy returns of tomorrow, and give her the doll.'

'I won't let the little beast kiss me,' stipulated Victor.

His mother said nothing; Victor had not been half as troublesome as she had anticipated. When he chose he could really be dreadfully naughty.

Emmeline and Bert were just moving away from the window when Morlvera made her exit from the shop, very carefully held in Victor's arms. A look of sinister triumph seemed to glow in her hard, inquisitorial face. As for Victor, a certain scornful serenity had replaced the earlier scowls; he had evidently accepted defeat with a contemptuous good grace.

The tall lady gave a direction to the footman and settled herself in the carriage. The little figure in the white sailor suit clambered in beside her, still carefully holding the elegantly garbed doll.

The car had to be backed a few yards in the process of turning. Very stealthily, very gently, very mercilessly Victor sent Morlvera flying over his shoulder, so that she fell into the road just behind the retrogressing wheel. With a soft, pleasant-sounding scrunch the car went over the prostrate form, then it moved forward again with another scrunch. The carriage moved off and left Bert and Emmeline gazing in scared delight at a sorry mess of petrol-smeared velvet, sawdust, and leopard-skin, which was all that remained of the hateful Morlvera. They gave a shrill cheer, and then raced away shuddering from the scene of so much rapidly enacted tragedy.

Later that afternoon, when they were engaged in the pursuit of minnows by the waterside in St James's Park, Emmeline said in a solemn undertone to Bert—

'I've bin finking. Do you know oo 'e was? 'E was 'er little boy wot she'd sent away to live wiv poor folks. 'E come back and done that.'

The Romancers

It was autumn in London, that blessed season between the harshness of winter and the insincerities of summer; a trustful season when one buys bulbs and sees to the registration of one's vote, believing perpetually in spring and a change of Government.

Morton Crosby sat on a bench in a secluded corner of Hyde Park, lazily enjoying a cigarette and watching the slow grazing promenade of a pair of snow-geese, the male looking rather like an albino edition of the russet-hued female. Out of the corner of his eye Crosby also noted with some interest the hesitating hoverings of a human figure, which had passed and repassed his seat two or three times at shortening intervals, like a wary crow about to alight near some possibly edible morsel. Inevitably the figure came to an anchorage on the bench, within easy talking distance of its original occupant. The uncared-for clothes, the aggressive, grizzled beard, and the furtive, evasive eye of the new-comer bespoke the professional cadger, the man who would undergo hours of humiliating tale-spinning and rebuff rather than adventure on half a day's decent work.

For a while the new-comer fixed his eyes straight in front of him in a strenuous, unseeing gaze; then his voice broke out with the insinuating inflection of one who has a story to retail well worth any loiterer's while to listen to.

'It's a strange world,' he said.

As the statement met with no response he altered it to the form of a question.

'I dare say you've found it to be a strange world, mister?'

'As far as I am concerned,' said Crosby, 'the strangeness has worn off in the course of thirty-six years.'

'Ah,' said the greybeard, 'I could tell you things that you'd hardly believe. Marvellous things that have really happened to me.'

'Nowadays there is no demand for marvellous things that have really happened,' said Crosby discouragingly; 'the professional writers of fiction turn these things out so much better. For instance, my neighbours tell me wonderful, incredible things that their Aberdeens and chows and borzois have done; I never listen to them. On the other hand, I have read *The Hound of the Baskervilles* three times.'

The greybeard moved uneasily in his seat; then he opened up new country.

'I take it that you are a professing Christian,' he observed.

'I am a prominent and I think I may say an influential member of the Mussulman community of Eastern Persia,' said Crosby, making an excursion himself into the realms of fiction.

The greybeard was obviously disconcerted at this new check of introductory conversation, but the defeat was only momentary.

'Persia. I should never have taken you for a Persian,' he remarked, with a somewhat aggrieved air.

'I am not,' said Crosby; 'my father was an Afghan.'

'An Afghan!' said the other, smitten into bewildered silence for a moment. Then he recovered himself and renewed his attack.

'Afghanistan. Ah! We've had some wars with that country; now, I dare say, instead of fighting it we might have learned something from it. A very wealthy country, I believe. No real poverty there.'

He raised his voice on the word 'poverty' with a suggestion of intense feeling. Crosby saw the opening and avoided it.

'It possesses, nevertheless, a number of highly talented and ingenious beggars,' he said; 'if I had not spoken so disparagingly of marvellous things that have really happened I would tell you the story of Ibrahim and the eleven camel-loads of blotting-paper. Also I have forgotten exactly how it ended.'

'My own life-story is a curious one,' said the stranger,

apparently stifling all desire to hear the history of Ibrahim; 'I was not always as you see me now.'

'We are supposed to undergo complete change in the course of every seven years,' said Crosby, as an explanation of the foregoing announcement.

'I mean I was not always in such distressing circumstances as I am at present,' pursued the stranger doggedly.

'That sounds rather rude,' said Crosby stiffly, 'considering that you are at present talking to a man reputed to be one of the most gifted conversationalists of the Afghan border.'

'I don't mean in that way,' said the greybeard hastily; 'I've been very much interested in your conversation. I was alluding to my unfortunate financial position. You mayn't hardly believe it, but at the present moment I am absolutely without a farthing. Don't see any prospect of getting any money, either, for the next few days. I don't suppose you've ever found yourself in such a position,' he added.

'In the town of Yom,' said Crosby, 'which is in Southern Afghanistan, and which also happens to be my birthplace, there was a Chinese philosopher who used to say that one of the three chief human blessings was to be absolutely without money. I forget what the other two were.'

'Ah, I dare say,' said the stranger, in a tone that betrayed no enthusiasm for the philosopher's memory; 'and did he practise what he preached? That's the test.'

'He lived happily with very little money or resources,' said Crosby.

'Then I expect he had friends who would help him liberally whenever he was in difficulties, such as I am in at present.'

'In Yom,' said Crosby, 'it is not necessary to have friends in order to obtain help. Any citizen of Yom would help a stranger as a matter of course.'

The greybeard was now genuinely interested. The conversation had at last taken a favourable turn.

'If someone, like me, for instance, who was in undeserved

difficulties, asked a citizen of that town you speak of for a small loan to tide over a few days' impecuniosity – five shillings, or perhaps a rather larger sum – would it be given to him as a matter of course?'

'There would be a certain preliminary,' said Crosby; 'one would take him to a wine-shop and treat him to a measure of wine, and then after a little high-flown conversation, one would put the desired sum in his hand and wish him good-day. It is a roundabout way of performing a simple transaction, but in the East all ways are roundabout.'

The listener's eyes were glittering.

'Ah,' he exclaimed, with a thin sneer ringing meaningly through his words, 'I suppose you've given up all those generous customs since you left your town. Don't practise them now, I expect.'

'No one who has lived in Yom,' said Crosby fervently, 'and remembers its green hills covered with apricot and almond trees, and the cold water that rushes down like a caress from the upland snows and dashes under the little wooden bridges, no one who remembers these things and treasures the memory of them would ever give up a single one of its unwritten laws and customs. To me they are as binding as though I still lived in that hallowed home of my youth.'

'Then if I was to ask you for a small loan—' began the grey-beard fawningly, edging nearer on the seat and hurriedly wondering how large he might safely make his request, 'if I was to ask you for, say—'

'At any other time, certainly,' said Crosby; 'in the months of November and December, however, it is absolutely forbidden for any one of our race to give or receive loans or gifts; in fact, one does not willingly speak of them. It is considered unlucky. We will therefore close this discussion.'

'But it is still October!' exclaimed the adventurer with an eager, angry whine, as Crosby rose from his seat; 'wants eight days to the end of the month!'

'The Afghan November began yesterday,' said Crosby severely, and in another moment he was striding across the Park, leaving his recent companion scowling and muttering furiously on the seat.

'I don't believe a word of his story,' he chattered to himself; 'pack of nasty lies from beginning to end. Wish I'd told him so to his face. Calling himself an Afghan.'

The snorts and snarls that escaped from him for the next quarter of an hour went far to support the truth of the old saying that two of a trade never agree.

REPERCUSSIONS

You Were Perfectly Fine

THE pale young man eased himself carefully into the low chair, and rolled his head to the side, so that the cool chintz comforted his cheek and temple.

'Oh, dear,' he said. 'Oh, dear, oh, dear, oh, dear. Oh.'

The clear-eyed girl, sitting light and erect on the couch, smiled brightly at him.

'Not feeling so well today?' she said.

'Oh, I'm great,' he said. 'Corking, I am. Know what time I got up? Four o'clock this afternoon, sharp. I kept trying to make it, and every time I took my head off the pillow, it would roll under the bed. This isn't my head I've got on now. I think this is something that used to belong to Walt Whitman. Oh, dear, oh, dear, oh, dear.'

'Do you think maybe a drink would make you feel better?' she said.

'The hair of the mastiff that bit me?' he said. 'Oh, no, thank you. Please never speak of anything like that again. I'm through. I'm all, all through. Look at that hand; steady as a humming-bird. Tell me, was I very terrible last night?'

'Oh, goodness,' she said, 'everybody was feeling pretty high. You were all right.'

'Yeah,' he said. 'I must have been dandy. Is everybody sore at me?'

'Good heavens, no,' she said. 'Everyone thought you were terribly funny. Of course, Jim Pierson was a little stuffy, there, for a minute at dinner. But people sort of held him back in his chair, and got him calmed down. I don't think anybody at the other tables noticed it at all. Hardly anybody.'

'He was going to sock me?' he said. 'Oh, Lord. What did I do to him?'

'Why, you didn't do a thing,' she said. 'You were perfectly fine. But you know how silly Jim gets, when he thinks anybody is making too much fuss over Elinor.'

'Was I making a pass at Elinor?' he said. 'Did I do that?'

'Of course you didn't,' she said. 'You were only fooling, that's all. She thought you were awfully amusing. She was having a marvellous time. She only got a little tiny bit annoyed just once, when you poured the clam-juice down her back.'

'My God,' he said. 'Clam-juice down that back. And every vertebra a little Cabot. Dear God. What'll I ever do?'

'Oh, she'll be all right,' she said. 'Just send her some flowers, or something. Don't worry about it. It isn't anything.'

'No, I won't worry,' he said. 'I haven't got a care in the world. I'm sitting pretty. Oh, dear, oh, dear. Did I do any other fascinating tricks at dinner?'

'You were fine,' she said. 'Don't be so foolish about it. Everybody was crazy about you. The maître d'hôtel was a little worried because you wouldn't stop singing, but he really didn't mind. All he said was, he was afraid they'd close the place again, if there was so much noise. But he didn't care a bit, himself. I think he loved seeing you have such a good time. Oh, you were just singing away, there, for about an hour. It wasn't so terribly loud, at all.'

'So I sang,' he said. 'That must have been a treat. I sang.'

'Don't you remember?' she said. 'You just sang one song after another. Everybody in the place was listening. They loved it. Only you kept insisting that you wanted to sing some song about some kind of fusiliers or other, and everybody kept shushing you, and you'd keep trying to start it again. You were wonderful. We were all trying to make you stop singing for a minute, and eat something, but you wouldn't hear of it. My, you were funny.'

'Didn't I eat any dinner?' he said.

'Oh, not a thing,' she said. 'Every time the waiter would offer you something, you'd give it right back to him, because you said that he was your long-lost brother, changed in the cradle by a gipsy band, and that anything you had was his. You had him simply roaring at you.'

'I bet I did,' he said. 'I bet I was comical. Society's Pet, I must have been. And what happened then, after my overwhelming success with the waiter?'

'Why, nothing much,' she said. 'You took a sort of dislike to some old man with white hair, sitting across the room, because you didn't like his necktie and you wanted to tell him about it. But we got you out, before he got really mad.'

'Oh, we got out,' he said. 'Did I walk?'

'Walk! Of course you did,' she said. 'You were absolutely all right. There was that nasty stretch of ice on the sidewalk, and you did sit down awfully hard, you poor dear. But good heavens, that might have happened to anybody.'

'Oh, sure,' he said. 'Louisa Alcott or anybody. So I fell down on the sidewalk. That would explain what's the matter with my— Yes. I see. And then what, if you don't mind?'

'Ah, now, Peter!' she said. 'You can't sit there and say you don't remember what happened after that! I did think that maybe you were just a little tight at dinner – oh, you were perfectly all right, and all that, but I did know you were feeling pretty gay. But you were so serious, from the time you fell down – I never knew you to be that way. Don't you know, how you told me I had never seen your real self before? Oh, Peter, I just couldn't bear it, if you didn't remember that lovely long ride we took together in the taxi! Please, you do remember that, don't you? I think it would simply kill me, if you didn't.'

'Oh, yes,' he said. 'Riding in the taxi. Oh, yes, sure. Pretty long ride, hmm?'

'Round and round and round the park,' she said. 'Oh, and the trees were shining so in the moonlight. And you said you never knew before that you really had a soul.'

'Yes,' he said. 'I said that. That was me.'

'You said such lovely, lovely things,' she said. 'And I'd never known, all this time, how you had been feeling about me, and I'd never dared to let you see how I felt about you. And then last night – oh, Peter dear, I think that taxi ride was the most important thing that ever happened to us in our lives.'

'Yes,' he said. 'I guess it must have been.'

'And we're going to be so happy,' she said. 'Oh, I just want to tell everybody! But I don't know – I think maybe it would be sweeter to keep it all to ourselves.'

'I think it would be,' he said.

'Isn't it lovely?' she said.

'Yes,' he said. 'Great.'

'Lovely!' she said.

'Look here,' he said, 'do you mind if I have a drink? I mean, just medicinally, you know. I'm off the stuff for life, so help me. But I think I feel a collapse coming on.'

'Oh, I think it would do you good,' she said. 'You poor boy, it's a shame you feel so awful. I'll go make you a whisky and soda.'

'Honestly,' he said, 'I don't see how you could ever want to speak to me again, after I made such a fool of myself, last night. I think I'd better go join a monastery in Tibet.'

'You crazy idiot,' she said. 'As if I could ever let you go away now! Stop talking like that. You were perfectly fine.'

She jumped up from the couch, kissed him quickly on the forehead, and ran out of the room.

The pale young man looked after her and shook his head long and slowly, then dropped it in his damp and trembling hands.

'Oh, dear,' he said. 'Oh, dear, oh, dear, oh, dear.'

Sredni Vashtar

CONRADIN was ten years old, and the doctor had pronounced his professional opinion that the boy would not live another five years. The doctor was silky and effete, and counted for little, but his opinion was endorsed by Mrs De Ropp, who counted for nearly everything. Mrs De Ropp was Conradin's cousin and guardian, and in his eyes she represented those three-fifths of the world that are necessary and disagreeable and real; the other two-fifths, in perpetual antagonism to the foregoing, were summed up in himself and his imagination. One of these days Conradin supposed he would succumb to the mastering pressure of wearisome necessary things – such as illnesses and coddling restrictions and drawn-out dullness. Without his imagination, which was rampant under the spur of loneliness, he would have succumbed long ago.

Mrs De Ropp would never, in her honestest moments, have confessed to herself that she disliked Conradin, though she might have been dimly aware that thwarting him 'for his good' was a duty which she did not find particularly irksome. Conradin hated her with a desperate sincerity which he was perfectly able to mask. Such few pleasure as he could contrive for himself gained an added relish from the likelihood that they would be displeasing to his guardian, and from the realm of his imagination she was locked out – an unclean thing, which should find no entrance.

In the dull, cheerless garden, overlooked by so many windows that were ready to open with a message not to do this or that, or a reminder that medicines were due, he found little attraction. The few fruit-trees that it contained were set jealously apart from his plucking, as though they were rare specimens of their kind blooming in an arid waste; it would probably have been difficult to find a market-gardener who would have offered ten shillings for their entire yearly produce. In a forgotten corner, however, almost hidden behind a dismal shrubbery, was a disused tool-shed of respectable proportions, and within its walls Conradin found a haven, something that took on the varying aspects of a playroom and a cathedral. He had peopled it with a legion of familiar phantoms, evoked partly from fragments of history and partly from his own brain, but it also boasted two inmates of flesh and blood. In one corner lived a ragged-plumaged Houdan hen, on which the boy lavished an affection that had scarcely another outlet. Further back in the gloom stood a large hutch, divided into two compartments, one of which was fronted with close iron bars. This was the abode of a large polecat-ferret, which a friendly butcher-boy had once smuggled, cage and all, into its present quarters, in exchange for a long-secreted hoard of small silver. Conradin was dreadfully afraid of the lithe, sharp-fanged beast, but it was his most treasured possession. Its very presence in the tool-shed was a secret and fearful joy, to be kept scrupulously from the knowledge of the Woman, as he privately dubbed his cousin. And one day, out of Heaven knows what material, he spun the beast a wonderful name, and from that moment it grew into a god and a religion. The Woman indulged in religion once a week at a church near by, and took Conradin with her, but to him the church service was an alien rite in the House of Rimmon. Every Thursday, in the dim and musty silence of the tool-shed, he worshipped with mystic and elaborate ceremonial before the wooden hutch where dwelt Sredni Vashtar, the great ferret. Red flowers in their season and scarlet berries in the winter-time were offered at his shrine, for he was a god who laid some special stress on the fierce impatient side of things, as opposed to the Woman's religion, which, as far as Conradin could observe, went to great lengths in the contrary direction. And on great festivals powdered nutmeg was strewn in front of his hutch, an important feature of the offering being that the nutmeg had to be stolen. These festivals were of irregular occurrence, and were chiefly appointed to celebrate some passing event. On one occasion, when Mrs De Ropp suffered from acute toothache for three days, Conradin kept up the festival during the entire three days, and almost succeeded in persuading himself that Sredni Vashtar was personally responsible for the toothache. If the malady had lasted for another day the supply of nutmeg would have given out.

The Houdan hen was never drawn into the cult of Sredni Vashtar. Conradin had long ago settled that she was an Anabaptist. He did not pretend to have the remotest knowledge as to what an Anabaptist was, but he privately hoped that it was dashing and not very respectable. Mrs De Ropp was the ground plan on which he based and detested all respectability.

After a while Conradin's absorption in the tool-shed began to attract the notice of his guardian. 'It is not good for him to be pottering down there in all weathers,' she promptly decided, and at breakfast one morning she announced that the Houdan hen had been sold and taken away overnight. With her short-sighted eyes she peered at Conradin, waiting for an outbreak of rage and sorrow, which she was ready to rebuke with a flow of excellent precepts and reasoning. But Conradin said nothing: there was nothing to be said. Something perhaps in his white set face gave her a momentary qualm, for at tea that afternoon there was toast on the table, a delicacy which she usually banned on the ground that it was bad for him; also because the making of it 'gave trouble', a deadly offence in the middle-class feminine eye.

'I thought you liked toast,' she exclaimed, with an injured air, observing that he did not touch it.

'Sometimes,' said Conradin.

In the shed that evening there was an innovation in the worship of the hutch-god. Conradin had been wont to chant his praises, tonight he asked a boon.

'Do one thing for me, Sredni Vashtar.'

The thing was not specified. As Sredni Vashtar was a god he must be supposed to know. And choking back a sob as he looked at that other empty corner, Conradin went back to the world he so hated.

And every night, in the welcome darkness of his bedroom, and every evening in the dusk of the tool-shed, Conradin's bitter litany went up: 'Do one thing for me, Sredni Vashtar.'

Mrs De Ropp noticed that the visits to the shed did not cease, and one day she made a further journey of inspection.

'What are you keeping in that locked hutch?' she asked. 'I believe it's guinea-pigs. I'll have them all cleared away.'

Conradin shut his lips tight, but the Woman ransacked his bedroom till she found the carefully hidden key, and forthwith marched down to the shed to complete her discovery. It was a cold afternoon, and Conradin had been bidden to keep to the house. From the furthest window of the dining-room the door of the shed could just be seen beyond the corner of the shrubbery, and there Conradin stationed himself. He saw the Woman enter, and then he imagined her opening the door of the sacred hutch and peering down with her short-sighted eyes into the thick straw bed where his god lay hidden. Perhaps she would prod at the straw in her clumsy impatience. And Conradin fervently breathed his prayer for the last time. But he knew as he prayed that he did not believe. He knew that the Woman would come out presently with that pursed smile he loathed so well on her face, and that in an hour or two the gardener would carry away his wonderful god, a god no longer, but a simple brown ferret in a hutch. And he knew that the Woman would triumph always as she triumphed now, and that he would grow ever more sickly under her pestering and domineering and superior wisdom, till one day nothing would matter much more with him, and the doctor would be proved right. And in the sting and misery of his defeat, he began to chant loudly and defiantly the hymn of his threatened idol:

Sredni Vashtar went forth,
His thoughts were red thoughts and his teeth were white.
His enemies called for peace, but he brought them death.
Sredni Vashtar the Beautiful.

And then of a sudden he stopped his chanting and drew closer to the window-pane. The door of the shed still stood ajar as it had been left, and the minutes were slipping by. They were long minutes, but they slipped by nevertheless. He watched the starlings running and flying in little parties across the lawn; he counted them over and over again, with one eye always on that swinging door. A sour-faced maid came in to lay the table for tea, and still Conradin stood and waited and watched. Hope had crept by inches into his heart, and now a look of triumph began to blaze in his eyes that had only known the wistful patience of defeat. Under his breath, with a furtive exultation, he began once again the paean of victory and devastation. And presently his eyes were rewarded; out through that doorway came a long, low, yellow-and-brown beast, with eyes a-blink at the waning daylight, and dark wet stains around the fur of jaws and throat. Conradin dropped on his knees. The great polecat-ferret made its way down to a small brook at the foot of the garden, drank for a moment, then crossed a little plank bridge and was lost to sight in the bushes. Such was the passing of Sredni Vashtar.

'Tea is ready,' said the sour-faced maid; 'where is the mistress?'

'She went down to the shed some time ago,' said Conradin.

And while the maid went to summon her mistress to tea, Conradin fished a toasting-fork out of the sideboard drawer and proceeded to toast himself a piece of bread. And during the toasting of it and the buttering of it with much butter and the slow enjoyment of eating it, Conradin listened to the noises and silences which fell in quick spasms beyond the dining-room door. The loud foolish screaming of the maid, the answering chorus of wondering ejaculations from the kitchen region, the scuttering footsteps and hurried embassies for outside help, and, then, after a lull, the scared sobbings and the shuffling tread of those who bore a heavy burden into the house.

'Whoever will break it to the poor child? I couldn't for the life of me!' exclaimed a shrill voice. And while they debated the matter among themselves, Conradin made himself another piece of toast.

The Lumber Room

THE children were to be driven, as a special treat, to the sands at Jagborough. Nicholas was not to be of the party; he was in disgrace. Only that morning he had refused to eat his wholesome bread-and-milk on the seemingly frivolous ground that there was a frog in it. Older and wiser and better people had told him that there could not possibly be a frog in his bread-and-milk and that he was not to talk nonsense; he continued, nevertheless, to talk what seemed the veriest nonsense, and described with much detail the coloration and markings of the alleged frog. The dramatic part of the incident was that there really was a frog in Nicholas' basin of bread-and-milk; he had put it there himself, so he felt entitled to know something about it. The sin of taking a frog from the garden and putting it into a bowl of wholesome bread-and-milk was enlarged on at great length, but the fact that stood out clearest in the whole affair, as it presented itself to the mind of Nicholas, was that the older, wiser, and better people had been proved to be profoundly in error in matters about which they had expressed the utmost assurance.

'You said there couldn't possibly be a frog in my bread-and-milk; there *was* a frog in my bread-and-milk,' he repeated, with the insistence of a skilled tactician who does not intend to shift from favourable ground.

So his boy-cousin and girl-cousin and his quite uninteresting younger brother were to be taken to Jagborough sands that afternoon and he was to stay at home. His cousins' aunt, who insisted, by an unwarranted stretch of imagination, in styling herself his aunt also, had hastily invented the Jagborough expedition in order to impress on Nicholas the delights that he had justly forfeited by his disgraceful conduct at the breakfast-table. It was her habit, whenever one of the children fell from grace, to improvise something of a festival nature from which the offender would be rigorously debarred; if all the children sinned collectively they were suddenly informed of a circus in a neighbouring town, a circus of unrivalled merit and uncounted elephants, to which, but for their depravity, they would have been taken that very day.

A few decent tears were looked for on the part of Nicholas when the moment for the departure of the expedition arrived. As a matter of fact, however, all the crying was done by his girl-cousin, who scraped her knee rather painfully against the step of the carriage as she was scrambling in.

'How she did howl,' said Nicholas cheerfully, as the party drove off without any of the elation of high spirits that should have characterized it.

'She'll soon get over that,' said the *soi-disant* aunt; 'it will be a glorious afternoon for racing about over those beautiful sands. How they will enjoy themselves!'

'Bobby won't enjoy himself much, and he won't race much either,' said Nicholas with a grim chuckle; 'his boots are hurting him. They're too tight.'

'Why didn't he tell me they were hurting?' asked the aunt with some asperity.

'He told you twice, but you weren't listening. You often don't listen when we tell you important things.'

'You are not to go into the gooseberry garden,' said the aunt, changing the subject.

'Why not?' demanded Nicholas.

'Because you are in disgrace,' said the aunt loftily.

Nicholas did not admit the flawlessness of the reasoning; he felt perfectly capable of being in disgrace and in a gooseberry garden at the same moment. His face took on an expression of considerable obstinacy. It was clear to his aunt that he was determined to get into the gooseberry garden, 'only,' as she remarked to herself, 'because I have told him he is not to.'

Now the gooseberry garden had two doors by which it might be entered, and once a small person like Nicholas could slip in there he could effectually disappear from view amid the masking growth of artichokes, raspberry canes, and fruit bushes. The aunt had many other things to do that afternoon, but she spent an hour or two in trivial gardening operations among flower beds and shrubberies, whence she could keep a watchful eye on the two doors that led to the forbidden paradise. She was a woman of few ideas, with immense powers of concentration.

Nicholas made one or two sorties into the front garden, wriggling his way with obvious stealth of purpose towards one or other of the doors, but never able for a moment to evade the aunt's watchful eye. As a matter of fact, he had no intention of trying to get into the gooseberry garden, but it was extremely convenient for him that his aunt should believe that he had; it was a belief that would keep her on self-imposed sentry-duty for the greater part of the afternoon. Having thoroughly confirmed and fortified her suspicions, Nicholas slipped back into the house and rapidly put into execution a plan of action that had long germinated in his brain. By standing on a chair in the library one could reach a shelf on which reposed a fat, important-looking key. The key was as important as it looked; it was the instrument which kept the mysteries of the lumber-room secure from unauthorized intrusion, which opened a way only for aunts and such-like privileged persons. Nicholas had not had much experience of the art of fitting keys into keyholes and turning locks, but for some days past he had practised with the key of the schoolroom door; he did not believe in trusting too much to luck and accident. The key turned stiffly in the lock, but it turned. The door opened, and Nicholas was in an unknown land, compared with which the gooseberry garden was a stale delight, a mere material pleasure.

Often and often Nicholas had pictured to himself what the lumber-room might be like, that region that was so carefully sealed from youthful eyes and concerning which no questions were ever answered. It came up to his expectations. In the first place it was large and dimly lit, one high window opening on to the forbidden garden being its only source of illumination. In the second place it was a storehouse of unimagined treasures. The aunt-by-assertion was one of those people who think that things spoil by use and consign them to dust and damp by way of preserving them. Such parts of the house as Nicholas knew best were rather bare and cheerless, but here there were wonderful things for the eye to feast on. First and foremost there was a piece of framed tapestry that was evidently meant to be a fire-screen. To Nicholas it was a living, breathing story; he sat down on a roll of Indian hangings, glowing in wonderful colours beneath a layer of dust, and took in all the details of the tapestry picture. A man, dressed in the hunting costume of some remote period, had just transfixed a stag with an arrow; it could not have been a difficult shot because the stag was only one or two paces away from him; in the thickly growing vegetation that the picture suggested it would not have been difficult to creep up to a feeding stag, and the two spotted dogs that were springing forward to join in the chase had evidently been trained to keep to heel till the arrow was discharged. That part of the picture was simple, if interesting, but did the huntsman see, what Nicholas saw, that four galloping wolves were coming in his direction through the wood? There might be more than four of them hidden behind the trees, and in any case would the man and his dogs be able to cope with the four wolves if they made an attack? The man had only two arrows left in his quiver, and he might miss with one or both of them; all one knew about his skill in shooting was that he could hit a large stag at a ridiculously short range. Nicholas sat for many golden minutes revolving the possibilities of the scene; he was inclined to think that there were more than four wolves and that the man and his dogs were in a tight corner.

But there were other objects of delight and interest claiming his instant attention; there were quaint twisted candlesticks in the shape of snakes, and a teapot fashioned like a china duck, out of whose open beak the tea was supposed to come. How dull and shapeless the nursery teapot seemed in comparison! And there was a carved sandal-wood box packed tight with aromatic cotton-wool, and between the layers of cotton-wool were little brass figures, hump-necked bulls, and peacocks and goblins, delightful to see and to handle. Less promising in appearance was a large square book with plain black covers; Nicholas peeped into it, and, behold, it was full of coloured pictures of birds. And such birds! In the garden, and in the lanes when he went for a walk, Nicholas came across a few birds, of which the largest were an occasional magpie or wood-pigeon; here were herons and bustards, kites, toucans, tiger-bitterns, brush turkeys, ibises, golden pheasants, a whole portrait gallery of undreamed-of creatures. And as he was admiring the colouring of the mandarin duck and assigning a life-history to it, the voice of his aunt in shrill vociferation of his name came from the gooseberry garden without. She had grown suspicious of his long disappearance, and had leapt to the conclusion that he had climbed over the wall behind the sheltering screen of the lilac bushes; she was now engaged in energetic and rather hopeless search for him among the artichokes and raspberry canes.

'Nicholas, Nicholas!' she screamed, 'you are to come out of this at once. It's no use trying to hide there; I can see you all the time.'

It was probably the first time for twenty years that anyone had smiled in that lumber-room.

Presently the angry repetitions of Nicholas' name gave way to a shriek, and a cry for somebody to come quickly. Nicholas shut the book, restored it carefully to its place in a corner, and shook some dust from a neighbouring pile of newspapers over it. Then he crept from the room, locked the door, and replaced the key exactly where he had found it. His aunt was still calling his name when he sauntered into the front garden.

'Who's calling?' he asked.

'Me,' came the answer from the other side of the wall; 'didn't you hear me? I've been looking for you in the gooseberry garden, and I've slipped into the rain-water tank. Luckily there's no water in it, but the sides are slippery and I can't get out. Fetch the little ladder from under the cherry tree—'

'I was told I wasn't to go into the gooseberry garden,' said Nicholas promptly.

'I told you not to, and now I tell you that you may,' came the voice from the rain-water tank, rather impatiently.

'Your voice doesn't sound like aunt's,' objected Nicholas; 'you may be the Evil One tempting me to be disobedient. Aunt often tells me that the Evil One tempts me and that I always yield. This time I'm not going to yield.'

'Don't talk nonsense,' said the prisoner in the tank; 'go and fetch the ladder.'

'Will there be strawberry jam for tea?' asked Nicholas innocently.

'Certainly there will be,' said the aunt, privately resolving that Nicholas should have none of it.

'Now I know that you are the Evil One and not aunt,' shouted Nicholas gleefully; 'when we asked aunt for strawberry jam yesterday she said there wasn't any. I know there are four jars of it in the store cupboard, because I looked, and of course you know it's there, but *she* doesn't, because she said there wasn't any. Oh, Devil, you *have* sold yourself!'

There was an unusual sense of luxury in being able to talk to an aunt as though one was talking to the Evil One, but Nicholas knew, with childish discernment, that such luxuries were not to be over-indulged in. He walked noisily away, and it was a kitchen-maid, in search of parsley, who eventually rescued the aunt from the rain-water tank.

Tea that evening was partaken of in a fearsome silence. The tide had been at its highest when the children had arrrived at Jagborough Cove, so there had been no sands to play on, a circumstance that the aunt had overlooked in the haste of organizing her punitive expedition. The tightness of Bobby's boots had had disastrous effect on his temper the whole of the afternoon, and altogether the children could not have been said to have enjoyed themselves. The aunt maintained the frozen muteness of one who has suffered undignified and unmerited detention in a rain-water tank for thirty-five minutes. As for Nicholas, he, too, was silent, in the absorption of one who has much to think about; it was just possible, he considered, that the huntsman would escape with his hounds while the wolves feasted on the stricken stag.

FACADES

Arrangement in Black and White

THE woman with the pink velvet poppies twined round the assisted gold of her hair traversed the crowded room at an interesting gait combining a skip with a sidle, and clutched the lean arm of her host.

'Now I got you!' she said. 'Now you can't get away!'

'Why, hello,' said her host. 'Well. How are you?'

'Oh, I'm finely,' she said. 'Just simply finely. Listen. I want you to do me the most terrible favour. Will you? Will you please? Pretty please?'

'What is it?' said her host.

'Listen,' she said. 'I want to meet Walter Williams. Honestly, I'm just simply crazy about that man. Oh, when he sings! When he sings those spirituals! Well, I said to Burton, "It's a good thing for you Walter Williams is coloured," I said, "or you'd have lots of reason to be jealous." I'd really love to meet him. I'd like to tell him I've heard him sing. Will you be an angel and introduce me to him?'

'Why, certainly,' said her host. 'I thought you'd met him. The party's for him. Where is he, anyway?'

'He's over there by the bookcase,' she said. 'Let's wait till those people get through talking to him. Well, I think you're simply marvellous, giving this perfectly marvellous party for him, and having him meet all these white people, and all. Isn't he terribly grateful?'

'I hope not,' said her host.

'I think it's really terribly nice,' she said. 'I do. I don't see why on earth it isn't perfectly all right to meet coloured people. I haven't any feeling at all about it – not one single bit. Burton –

oh, he's just the other way. Well, you know, he comes from Virginia, and you know how they are.'

'Did he come tonight?' said her host.

'No, he couldn't,' she said. 'I'm a regular grass widow tonight. I told him when I left, "There's no telling what I'll do," I said. He was just so tired out, he couldn't move. Isn't it a shame?'

'Ah,' said her host.

'Wait till I tell him I met Walter Williams!' she said. 'He'll just about die. Oh, we have more arguments about coloured people. I talk to him like I don't know what, I get so excited. "Oh, don't be so silly," I say. But I must say for Burton, he's heaps broader-minded than lots of these Southerners. He's really awfully fond of coloured people. Well, he says himself, he wouldn't have white servants. And you know, he had this old coloured nurse, this regular old nigger mammy, and he just simply loves her. Why, every time he goes home, he goes out in the kitchen to see her. He does, really, to this day. All he says is, he says he hasn't got a word to say against coloured people as long as they keep their place. He's always doing things for them – giving them clothes and I don't know what all. The only thing he says, he says he wouldn't sit down at the table with one for a million dollars. "Oh," I say to him, "you make me sick, talking like that." I'm just terrible to him. Aren't I terrible?'

'Oh, no, no, no,' said her host. 'No, no.'

'I am,' she said. 'I know I am. Poor Burton! Now, me, I don't feel that way at all. I haven't the slightest feeling about coloured people. Why, I'm just crazy about some of them. They're just like children – just as easy-going, and always singing and laughing and everything. Aren't they the happiest things you ever saw in your life? Honestly, it makes me laugh just to hear them. Oh, I like them. I really do. Well, now, listen, I have this coloured laundress, I've had her for years, and I'm devoted to her. She's a real character. And I want to tell you, I think of her as my friend. That's the way I think of her. As I say to Burton, "Well, for heaven's sakes, we're all human beings!" Aren't we?'

'Yes,' said her host. 'Yes, indeed.'

'Now this Walter Williams,' she said. 'I think a man like that's a real artist. I do. I think he deserves an awful lot of credit. Goodness, I'm so crazy about music or anything. I don't care *what* colour he is. I honestly think if a person's an artist, nobody ought to have any feeling at all about meeting them. That's absolutely what I say to Burton. Don't you think I'm right?'

'Yes,' said her host. 'Oh, yes.'

'That's the way I feel,' she said. 'I just can't understand people being narrow-minded. Why, I absolutely think it's a privilege to meet a man like Walter Williams. Yes, I do. I haven't any feeling at all. Well, my goodness, the good Lord made him, just the same as He did any of us. Didn't He?'

'Surely,' said her host. 'Yes, indeed.'

'That's what I say,' she said. 'Oh, I get so furious when people are narrow-minded about coloured people. It's just all I can do not to say something. Of course, I do admit when you get a bad coloured man, they're simply terrible. But as I say to Burton, there are some bad white people, too, in this world. Aren't there?'

'I guess there are,' said her host.

'Why, I'd really be glad to have a man like Walter Williams come to my house and sing for us, some time,' she said. 'Of course, I couldn't ask him on account of Burton, but I wouldn't have any feeling about it at all. Oh, can't he sing! Isn't it marvellous, the way they all have music in them? It just seems to be right *in* them. Come on, let's go on over and talk to him. Listen, what shall I do when I'm introduced? Ought I to shake hands? Or what?'

'Why, do whatever you want,' said her host.

'I guess maybe I'd better,' she said. 'I wouldn't for the world have him think I had any feeling. I think I'd better shake hands, just the way I would with anybody else. That's just exactly what I'll do.'

They reached the tall young Negro, standing by the bookcase. The host performed introductions; the Negro bowed.

'How do you do?' he said.

The woman with the pink velvet poppies extended her hand at the length of her arm and held it so for all the world to see, until the Negro took it, shook it, and gave it back to her.

'Oh, how do you do, Mr Williams,' she said. 'Well, how do you do. I've just been saying, I've enjoyed your singing so awfully much. I've been to your concerts, and we have you on the phonograph and everything. Oh, I just enjoy it!'

She spoke with great distinctness, moving her lips meticulously, as if in parlance with the deaf.

'I'm so glad,' he said.

'I'm just simply crazy about that *Water Boy* thing you sing.' she said. 'Honestly, I can't get it out of my head. I have my husband nearly crazy, the way I go around humming it all the time. Oh, he looks just as black as the ace of – Well. Tell me, where on earth do you ever get all those songs of yours? How do you ever get hold of them?'

'Why,' he said, 'there are so many different—'

'I should think you'd love singing them,' she said. 'It must be more fun. All those darling old spirituals – oh, I just love them! Well, what are you doing, now? Are you still keeping up your singing? Why don't you have another concert, some time?'

'I'm having one the sixteenth of this month,' he said.

'Well, I'll be there,' she said. 'I'll be there, if I possibly can. You can count on me. Goodness, here comes a whole raft of people to talk to you. You're just a regular guest of honour! Oh, who's that girl in white? I've seen her some place.'

'That's Katherine Burke,' said her host.

'Good Heavens,' she said, 'is that Katherine Burke? Why, she looks entirely different off the stage. I thought she was much better-looking. I had no idea she was so terribly dark. Why, she looks almost like – Oh, I think she's a wonderful actress! Don't you think she's a wonderful actress, Mr Williams? Oh, I think she's marvellous. Don't you?'

'Yes, I do,' he said.

'Oh, I do, too,' she said. 'Just wonderful. Well, goodness, we must give someone else a chance to talk to the guest of honour. Now, don't forget, Mr Williams, I'm going to be at that concert if I possibly can. I'll be there applauding like everything. And if I can't come, I'm going to tell everybody I know to go, anyway. Don't you forget!'

'I won't,' he said. 'Thank you so much.'

The host took her arm and piloted her into the next room.

'Oh, my dear,' she said. 'I nearly died! Honestly, I give you my word, I nearly passed away. Did you hear that terrible break I made? I was just going to say Katherine Burke looked almost like a nigger. I just caught myself in time. Oh, do you think he noticed?'

'I don't believe so,' said her host.

'Well, thank goodness,' she said, 'because I wouldn't have embarrassed him for anything. Why, he's awfully nice. Just as nice as he can be. Nice manners, and everything. You know, so many coloured people, you give them an inch, and they walk all over you. But he doesn't try any of that. Well, he's got more sense, I suppose. He's really nice. Don't you think so?'

'Yes,' said her host.

'I liked him,' she said. 'I haven't any feeling at all because he's a coloured man. I felt just as natural as I would with anybody. Talked to him just as naturally, and everything. But honestly, I could hardly keep a straight face. I kept thinking of Burton. Oh, wait till I tell Burton I called him "Mister"!'

The Chaplet

A STRANGE stillness hung over the restaurant; it was one of those rare moments when the orchestra was not discoursing the strains of the Ice-cream Sailor waltz.

'Did I ever tell you,' asked Clovis of his friend, 'the tragedy of music at mealtimes?

'It was a gala evening at the Grand Sybaris Hotel, and a special dinner was being served in the Amethyst dining-hall. The Amethyst dining-hall had almost a European reputation, especially with that section of Europe which is historically identified with the Jordan Valley. Its cooking was beyond reproach, and its orchestra was sufficiently highly salaried to be above criticism. Thither came in shoals the intensely musical and the almost intensely musical, who are very many, and in still greater numbers the merely musical, who know how Tschaikowsky's name is pronounced and can recognize several of Chopin's nocturnes if you give them due warning; these eat in the nervous, detached manner of roebuck feeding in the open, and keep anxious ears cocked towards the orchestra for the first hint of a recognizable melody.

' "Ah, yes, *Pagliacci*," they murmur, as the opening strains follow hot upon the soup, and if no contradiction is forthcoming from any better-informed quarter they break forth into subdued humming by way of supplementing the efforts of the musicians. Sometimes the melody starts on level terms with the soup, in which case the banqueters contrive somehow to hum between the spoonfuls; the facial expression of enthusiasts who are punctuating potage St Germain with *Pagliacci* is not beautiful, but it should be seen by those who are bent on observing all sides of life. One cannot discount the unpleasant things of this world merely by looking the other way.

'In addition to the aforementioned types the restaurant was patronized by a fair sprinkling of the absolutely non-musical; their presence in the dining-hall could only be explained on the supposition that they had come there to dine.

'The earlier stages of the dinner had worn off. The wine lists had been consulted, by some with the blank embarrassment of a schoolboy suddenly called on to locate a Minor Prophet in the tangled hinterland of the Old Testament, by others with the severe scrutiny which suggests that they have visited most of the higher-priced wines in their own homes and probed their family weaknesses. The diners who chose their wine in the latter fashion always gave their orders in a penetrating voice, with a plentiful garnishing of stage directions. By insisting on having your bottle pointing to the north when the cork is being drawn, or calling the waiter Max, you may induce an impression on your guests which hours of laboured boasting might be powerless to achieve. For this purpose, however, the guests must be chosen as carefully as the wine.

'Standing aside from the revellers in the shadow of a massive pillar was an interested spectator who was assuredly of the feast, and yet not in it. Monsieur Aristide Saucourt was the *chef* of the Grand Sybaris Hotel, and if he had an equal in his profession he had never acknowledged the fact. In his own domain he was a potentate, hedged around with the cold brutality that Genius expects rather than excuses in her children; he never forgave, and those who served him were careful that there should be little to forgive. In the outer world, the world which devoured his creations, he was an influence; how profound or how shallow an influence he never attempted to guess. It is the penalty and the safeguard of genius that it computes itself by troy weight in a world that measures by vulgar hundredweights.

'Once in a way the great man would be seized with a desire to watch the effects of his master-efforts, just as the guiding brain of Krupp's might wish at a supreme moment to intrude into the firing line of an artillery duel. And such an occasion was the present. For the first time in the history of the Grand Sybaris Hotel, he was presenting to its guests the dish which he had brought to that pitch of perfection which almost amounts to scandal. Canetons à la mode d'Amblève. In thin gilt lettering on the creamy white of the menu how little those words conveyed to the bulk of the imperfectly educated diners. And yet how much specialized effort had been lavished, how much carefully treasured lore had been ungarnered, before those six words could be written. In the Department of Deux-Sèvres ducklings had lived peculiar and beautiful lives and died in the odour of satiety to furnish the main theme of the dish; champignons, which even a purist for Saxon English would have hesitated to address as mushrooms, had contributed their languorous atrophied bodies to the garnishing, and a sauce devised in the twilight reign of the Fifteenth Louis had been summoned back from the imperishable past to take its part in the wonderful confection. Thus far had human effort laboured to achieve the desired result; the rest had been left to human genius – the genius of Aristide Saucourt.

'And now the moment had arrived for the serving of the great dish, the dish which world-weary Grand Dukes and market-obsessed money magnates counted among their happiest memories. And at the same moment something else happened. The leader of the highly salaried orchestra placed his violin caressingly against his chin, lowered his eyelids, and floated into a sea of melody.

' "Hark!" said most of the diners, "he is playing *The Chaplet.*"

'They knew it was *The Chaplet* because they had heard it played at luncheon and afternoon tea, and at supper the night before, and had not had time to forget.

' "Yes, he is playing *The Chaplet,*" they reassured one another. The general voice was unanimous on the subject. The orchestra had already played it eleven times that day, four times by desire and seven times from force of habit, but the familiar strains were greeted with the rapture due to a revelation. A murmur of much humming rose from half the tables in the room, and some of the more over-wrought listeners laid down knife and fork in order to be able to burst in with loud clappings at the earliest permissible moment.

'And the Canetons à la mode d'Amblève? In stupefied, sickened wonder Aristide watched them grow cold in total neglect, or suffer the almost worse indignity of perfunctory pecking and listless munching while the banqueters lavished their approval and applause on the music-makers. Calves' liver and bacon, with parsley sauce, could hardly have figured more ignominiously in the evening's entertainment. And while the master of culinary art leaned back against the sheltering pillar, choking with a horrible brain-searing rage that could find no outlet for its agony, the orchestra leader was bowing his acknowledgements of the hand-clappings that rose in a storm around him. Turning to his colleagues he nodded the signal for an encore. But before the violin had been lifted anew into position there came from the shadow of the pillar an explosive negative.

' "Noh! Noh! You do not play thot again!"

'The musician turned in furious astonishment. Had he taken warning from the look in the other man's eyes he might have acted differently. But the admiring plaudits were ringing in his ears, and he snarled out sharply, "That is for me to decide."

' "Noh! You play thot never again," shouted the *chef*, and the next moment he had flung himself violently upon the loathed being who had supplanted him in the world's esteem. A large metal tureen, filled to the brim with steaming soup, had just been placed on a side table in readiness for a late party of diners; before the waiting staff or the guests had time to realize what was happening, Aristide had dragged his struggling victim up to the table and plunged his head deep down into the almost boiling contents of the tureen. At the further end of the room the diners were still spasmodically applauding in view of an encore.

'Whether the leader of the orchestra died from drowning by

soup, or from the shock to his professional vanity, or was scalded to death, the doctors were never wholly able to agree. Monsieur Aristide Saucourt, who now lives in complete retirement, always inclined to the drowning theory.'

The Wolves of Cernogratz

'ARE there any old legends attached to the castle?' asked Conrad of his sister. Conrad was a prosperous Hamburg merchant, but he was the one poetically-dispositioned member of an eminently practical family.

The Baroness Gruebel shrugged her plump shoulders.

'There are always legends hanging about these old places. They are not difficult to invent and they cost nothing. In this case there is a story that when anyone dies in the castle all the dogs in the village and the wild beasts in the forest howl the night long. It would not be pleasant to listen to, would it?'

'It would be weird and romantic,' said the Hamburg merchant.

'Anyhow, it isn't true,' said the Baroness complacently; 'since we bought the place we have had proof that nothing of the sort happens. When the old mother-in-law died last springtime we all listened, but there was no howling. It is just a story that lends dignity to the place without costing anything.'

'The story is not as you have told it,' said Amalie, the grey old governess. Everyone turned and looked at her in astonishment. She was wont to sit silent and prim and faded in her place at table, never speaking unless someone spoke to her, and there were few who troubled themselves to make conversation with her. To-day a sudden volubility had descended on her; she continued to talk, rapidly and nervously, looking straight in front of her and seeming to address no one in particular.

'It is not when *anyone* dies in the castle that the howling is heard. It was when one of the Cernogratz family died here that the wolves came from far and near and howled at the edge of the forest just before the death hour. There were only a few couple of wolves that had their lairs in this part of the forest, but at such a time the keepers say there would be scores of them, gliding about in the shadows and howling in chorus, and the dogs of the castle and the village and all the farms round would bay and howl in fear and anger at the wolf chorus, and as the soul of the dying one left its body a tree would crash down in the park. That is what happened when a Cernogratz died in his family castle. But for a stranger dying here, of course no wolf would howl and no tree would fall. Oh, no.'

There was a note of defiance, almost of contempt, in her voice as she said the last words. The well-fed, much-too-well-dressed Baroness stared angrily at the dowdy old woman who had come forth from her usual and seemly position of effacement to speak so disrespectfully.

'You seem to know quite a lot about the von Cernogratz legends, Fräulein Schmidt,' she said sharply; 'I did not know that family histories were among the subjects you are supposed to be proficient in.'

The answer to her taunt was even more unexpected and astonishing than the conversational outbreak which had provoked it.

'I am a von Cernogratz myself,' said the old woman, 'that is why I know the family history.'

'You a von Cernogratz? You!' came in an incredulous chorus.

'When we became very poor,' she explained, 'and I had to go out and give teaching lessons, I took another name; I thought it would be more in keeping. But my grandfather spent much of his time as a boy in this castle, and my father used to tell me many stories about it, and, of course, I knew all the family legends and stories. When one has nothing left to one but memories, one guards and dusts them with especial care. I little thought when I took service with you that I should one day come with you to the old home of my family. I could wish it had been anywhere else.'

There was silence when she finished speaking, and then the Baroness turned the conversation to a less embarrassing topic than family histories. But afterwards, when the old governess had slipped away quietly to her duties, there arose a clamour of derision and disbelief.

'It was an impertinence,' snapped out the Baron, his protruding eyes taking on a scandalized expression; 'fancy the woman talking like that at our table. She almost told us we were nobodies, and I don't believe a word of it. She is just Schmidt and nothing more. She has been talking to some of the peasants about the old Cernogratz family, and raked up their history and their stories.'

'She wants to make herself out of some consequence,' said the Baroness; 'she knows she will soon be past work and she wants to appeal to our sympathies. Her grandfather, indeed!'

The Baroness had the usual number of grandfathers, but she never, never boasted about them.

'I dare say her grandfather was a pantry boy or something of the sort in the castle,' sniggered the Baron; 'that part of the story may be true.'

The merchant from Hamburg said nothing; he had seen tears in the old woman's eyes when she spoke of guarding her memories – or, being of an imaginative disposition, he thought he had.

'I shall give her notice to go as soon as the New Year festivities are over,' said the Baroness; 'till then I shall be too busy to manage without her.'

But she had to manage without her all the same, for in the cold biting weather after Christmas, the old governess fell ill and kept to her room.

'It is most provoking,' said the Baroness, as her guests sat round the fire on one of the last evenings of the dying year; 'all the time that she has been with us I cannot remember that she was ever seriously ill, too ill to go about and do her work, I mean. And now, when I have the house full, and she could be useful in so many ways, she goes and breaks down. One is sorry for her, of course, she looks so withered and shrunken, but it is intensely annoying all the same.'

'Most annoying,' agreed the banker's wife sympathetically; 'it is the intense cold, I expect, it breaks the old people up. It has been unusually cold this year.'

'The frost is the sharpest that has been known in December for many years,' said the Baron.

'And, of course, she is quite old,' said the Baroness; 'I wish I had given her notice some weeks ago, then she would have left before this happened to her. Why, Wappi, what is the matter with you?'

The small, woolly lapdog had leapt suddenly down from its cushion and crept shivering under the sofa. At the same moment an outburst of angry barking came from the dogs in the castle-yard, and other dogs could be heard yapping and barking in the distance.

'What is disturbing the animals?' asked the Baron.

And then the humans, listening intently, heard the sound that had roused the dogs to the demonstrations of fear and rage; heard a long-drawn whining howl, rising and falling, seeming at one moment leagues away, at others sweeping across the snow until it appeared to come from the foot of the castle walls. All the starved, cold misery of a frozen world, all the relentless hunger-fury of the wild, blended with other forlorn and haunting melodies to which one could give no name, seemed concentrated in that wailing cry.

'Wolves!' cried the Baron.

Their music broke forth in one raging burst, seeming to come from everywhere.

'Hundreds of wolves,' said the Hamburg merchant, who was a man of strong imagination.

Moved by some impulse which she could not have explained, the Baroness left her guests and made her way to the narrow, cheerless room where the old governess lay watching the hours of the dying year slip by. In spite of the biting cold of the winter night, the window stood open. With a scandalized exclamation on her lips, the Baroness rushed forward to close it.

'Leave it open,' said the old woman in a voice that for all its weakness carried an air of command such as the Baroness had never heard before from her lips.

'But you will die of cold!' she expostulated.

'I am dying in any case,' said the voice, 'and I want to hear their music. They have come from far and wide to sing the death-music of my family. It is beautiful that they have come; I am the last von Cernogratz that will die in our old castle, and they have come to sing to me. Hark, how loud they are calling!'

The cry of the wolves rose on the still winter air and floated round the castle walls in long-drawn piercing wails; the old woman lay back on her couch with a look of long-delayed happiness on her face.

'Go away,' she said to the Baroness; 'I am not lonely any more. I am one of a great old family. . . .'

'I think she is dying,' said the Baroness when she had rejoined her guests; 'I suppose we must send for a doctor. And that terrible howling! Not for much money would I have such death-music.'

'That music is not to be bought for any amount of money,' said Conrad.

'Hark! What is that other sound?' asked the Baron as a noise of splitting and crashing was heard.

It was a tree falling in the park.

There was a moment of constrained silence, and then the banker's wife spoke.

'It is the intense cold that is splitting the trees. It is also the cold that has brought the wolves out in such numbers. It is many years since we have had such a cold winter.'

The Baroness eagerly agreed that the cold was responsible for these things. It was the cold of the open window, too, which caused the heart failure that made the doctor's ministrations unnecessary for the old Fräulein. But the notice in the newspapers looked very well—

'On December 29th, at Schloss Cernogratz, Amalie von Cernogratz, for many years the valued friend of Baron and Baroness Gruebel.'

Follow-up Work

THE TRUTH

The Waltz (Parker)

Tobermory *and* Mrs Packletide's Tiger (Saki)

1. What was it, in each story, that each character was concealing, and why?
2. Are some of the truths here things that people *should* conceal, out of consideration for other people? Is there a case to be made for absolute honesty at all times? How would you define the kinds of things one should conceal?
3. In all three stories, the basic humour is in the contrast between people's private opinions and actions and their public behaviour. What other devices add to the sense of the ridiculous in each story? Are the characters exaggerated, for instance? Consider the incongruity of a cat who can talk suavely and yet fight the local tom, and so on.
4. How does each story suggest to the reader its particular period and setting? Do you find it easy to appreciate and enjoy a story with a setting outside your own experience or the world of today?
5. Which do you prefer, the colloquial style of the 'inner monologue' in 'The Waltz', or the slightly affected style of narration in the two stories by Saki? Contrast the two styles of writing.
6. Write a story of your own in which complications or embarrassment are caused by telling the whole truth. Consider someone who tells the truth in all circumstances, never leaving his opinions unsaid, contradicting even his superiors, showing no tact or consideration. Alternatively, work out a situation in which a child innocently blurts out some embarrassing information.

PATHETIC PEOPLE

Horsie (Parker)

The Sheep (Saki)

1. Pathos is the quality of arousing pity or sympathy; which of these two main characters arouses your pity more? Do you feel that either or both of them deserve your contempt? Do your feelings about them change in the course of reading each story?
2. Does Mr Gerald Cruger pity Miss Wilmarth at all? Has he any respect for her? Why does he buy her flowers? What does she think is the reason for this? Would *you* rather be pitied *or* held in contempt by other people?
3. Miss Wilmarth and the Sheep are both pitiful failures socially: does either of them realize this? Is either of them efficient or successful in any way at all? What do you think Kathleen saw in the Sheep as a future husband?
4. Why do the authors choose a horse and a sheep respectively to represent their characters? Could they have used other animals to suggest these particular characteristics? What other animals are used to suggest other human characteristics?
5. Is there some difference between these authors in their attitudes to their characters? Does either story become sentimental, with an exaggerated indulgence in feelings of pity? Does either author show true sentiment, genuine feelings of sympathy?
6. Write a character study of an imaginary person who is always at a disadvantage or in trouble. Include at least one anecdote to illustrate his personality in action. Before describing him, think carefully about your own attitude to him, and the attitudes of other people he has contact with.

DISCONTENTED

Too Bad (Parker)

The Mappined Life *and* The Philanthropist and the Happy Cat (Saki)

1. Examine and describe the causes of discontent in Mrs Weldon, Mrs Gurtleberry and Mrs Bessbury. What have they in common? Are they victims of a way of life that is too comfortable and too repetitive?
2. What kinds of men were the three husbands? Is each of them much to blame for his wife's discontent?
3. How far do you feel that the discontent of these women is a product of their social position – middle class wives with enough money and no careers or pressing responsibilities (such as young children)? Would you expect such dissatisfaction to become more widespread as more people have more leisure in the future?
4. Do any of these stories criticize the ways of life they describe, rather than giving an objective account of the situation? If so, how does this criticism become apparent? Is it stated openly, with the author giving his own opinion, or more subtly implied?
5. Discuss the narrative devices used in these stories: 'Too Bad' contrasts the internal with the external views of a marriage; 'The Mappined Life' and 'The Philanthropist and the Happy Cat' both make comparisons or contrasts between human and animal behaviour.
6. Either (a) Suggest how the discontent of any of these characters could have been cured. You could either put these thoughts down as an essay, or show this by continuing the stories.

Or (b) Write a composition discussing the ingredients of an ideal marriage, as you see them, in contrast with the dissatisfaction expressed here with a conventional, bourgeois marriage and home.

MARRIED LIFE

Here We Are (Parker)

The Reticence of Lady Anne (Saki)

1. Do you feel that the newly-wed couple in 'Here We Are' are almost searching for something to quarrel over? If so, why? Does their nervousness seem convincing and typical, or is this a rather conventional picture of people in this situation?

2. What kind of married relationship have Egbert and Lady Anne had, do you think? What kind of person is Egbert, judging from the way he talks and reasons? Can you imagine the couple in 'Here We Are' ending their married lives like Egbert and Lady Anne?

3. How far does the effect of each of these stories depend on its style, on the author's skill in description and realistic recording of conversation? Discuss the use of detail in each case. Which story seems more realistic? Could you imagine each story written by the other author, or have they each such a distinctive style that such an interchange would be impossible?

4. The narrative movement in 'Here We Are' is circular, while 'The Reticence of Lady Anne' leads up to an unexpected conclusion. Which seems the more effective ending for a short story? Is there a sense in which even the unexpected twist is consistent with the couple's character and relationship?

5. Many short stories fall into one of these two categories: the kind of story that relies on plot, often with a surprise ending, and the kind that has no very clear beginning or ending, but reveals character. Which technique do you prefer? Which is more typical of Parker and which of Saki? Apply the distinction as far as you can to all the stories in this selection.

6. Work out a conversation between two people thrown into close contact, such as when two strangers have to share a restaurant table, a theatre box, a taxi or a life-boat. Bring out personalities through dialogue and thoughts, rather than by commentary. Try to end the conversation with an unexpected twist at the end.

DISCOMFITURE

Clothe the Naked (Parker)

The Mouse *and* Dusk (Saki)

1. How far does Big Lannie in 'Clothe the Naked' seem typical of the very poor in her attitudes to (a) her own children, (b) Raymond, (c) charitable or official institutions, and (d) her employers? Does it make much difference that she is also a negro in pre-war America?

2. Why is the discomfiture of Raymond so much more moving than the embarrassment of Theodoric or the way in which Gortsby is fooled? What part is played by coincidence in each of these stories?

3. Does the attitude of Mrs Ewing to charity have anything in common with the attitude of Norman Gortsby? Why does each of them give something in the end? What are *your* feelings about working for charities, giving to 'good causes', and about beggars and others who pester people for a gift or a loan?

4. Compare and contrast the blind lady in the carriage (in 'The Mouse') with the blind child, Raymond (in 'Clothe the Naked').

5. Discuss the authors' attitudes to each of the following characters: Big Lannie, Raymond and Mrs Ewing in 'Clothe the Naked', Theodoric and the blind lady in 'The Mouse', and Norman Gortsby and the young man in 'Dusk'. Consider the ways in which the characters are described, and how the characters show the authors' attitudes. Is there an element of sentimentality in Dorothy Parker's attitude? Have the two authors different attitudes to poverty in these stories?

6. Write a story revolving around some experience of inadequacy or embarrassment. You could either choose a situation based upon an experience of your own, or develop a more contrived situation where a character suffers because he is blind or deaf or unable to speak the local language, or is taken in by some trick or fraud.

MAKE-BELIEVE

The Standard of Living (Parker)

Morlvera *and* The Romancers (Saki)

1. Discuss the way in which the make-believe in each of these stories is a defence against something. Why do the characters need to create fantasies for themselves in each story? How do their fantasies change or grow in each case?
2. Why do Midge and Annabel seem so upset by the price of the necklace? Are the children, Emmeline and Bert, equally disconcerted by the real fate of Morlvera? What is the cadger's reaction to Crosby's story in 'The Romancers'?
3. In what ways does Midge show more sensitivity and imagination than Annabel? Is the same true of Emmeline as compared with Bert? Is it imagination and quick-wittedness that allows Crosby to outwit his companion?
4. Are the characters in these stories equally serious about their own fantasies? Is it in some way necessary or important to be serious about make-believe?
5. What pleasure do people gain from make-believe? Is there a clear distinction between conscious story-telling, such as Crosby uses to gain his ends, and the kind of self-deception that sweeps the children along in 'Morlvera'? Which of the two categories does the fantasy built up by the girls in 'The Standard of Living' fall into? What pressure is there on them to play this game?
6. (a) Write a conversation in which two or more people together build up some kind of fantastic or impossible situation, each trying to outdo the other in invention or wit. The participants might be contrasted and shown as competing in their stories.

   (b) Write a story in which someone is building up a fantasy as a compensation for his own lack of money, success, friends, personality, intellect, skill or physique, and perhaps deceiving himself and others in doing so.

REPERCUSSIONS

You Were Perfectly Fine (Parker)

Sredni Vashtar *and* The Lumber Room (Saki)

1. What are the motives of the girl (in 'You Were Perfectly Fine'), Conradin and Nicholas? Compare and contrast them, considering what 'provocation' or other motivation there was in each situation.
2. How far do the three 'victims' deserve what they get in these stories? Is their 'punishment' only tolerable to us as readers because these are comically written short stories?
3. Do Nicholas and Conradin show signs of exceptional sensitivity and imagination? Are their fantasy lives characteristic of lonely and rather unhappy children?
4. Compare the various way in which the girl, Conradin and Nicholas each gains his or her ends. To what extent does each taunt or humiliate the 'victim', how far do they play upon other people's guilt or helplessness, and how far is the vengeance in the form of physical suffering? How far does each plan the course of events, and how far simply exploit propitious circumstances?
5. Judging from these and other stories in this selection, would you say that either of the two authors seems to be crueller, more biting in satire? Are these three particular stories typical of the work of the authors as represented in this selection?
6. Either (a) Write a short story in which someone finds an ingenious way to take his revenge for some injury.

   Or (b) Write a composition discussing the proposition that revenge can never be a satisfactory basis for justice.

FACADES

Arrangement in Black and White (Parker)

The Chaplet *and* The Wolves of Cernogratz (Saki)

1. Examine the attitude that the guest at the party has to Walter Williams. Whom is she trying to convince that she has no feelings against coloured people? How does she give her true feelings away? Is she herself aware of her prejudice and snobbery, and would it have been better if she both knew and openly spoke out her real feelings?
2. What exactly annoyed the *chef* when he exploded and attacked the leader of the orchestra? How does 'The Chaplet' make fun of people's false values?
3. Where does the false snobbery come out in 'The Wolves of Cernogratz'? Why do the family choose to put the notice in the newspapers in the form given at the end of the story?
4. Why is it wrong to be patronizing? Illustrate from these stories that harm can result from a false attitude of superiority to others. Which of the three 'victims' – Mr Williams, the *chef*, and Fräulein Schmidt – seems to be injured most clearly by the attitude of others to him or her?
5. Both Dorothy Parker and Saki make fun of people's false values and social snobbery. Do you find that one is more spiteful, more indignant, more scathing, than the other? Which of them seems to you more tolerant, or at least more cynical and resigned to such faults in human nature? Look back over the stories, and the other questions dealing with their attitudes as writers.
6. Imagine yourself as a victim of prejudice or snobbery, with others despising you for your parentage, the colour of your hair, or the way you dress, worship or behave. Describe your feelings about being treated as if you were odd, inferior, or even freakish.